Something Made of Vacuum

Other Books by Charles Ott:

The Floor of the World
A Science Fiction Adventure

A Weapon of Mathematics
A Fantasy Adventure

Something Made of Vacuum

by Charles Ott

Table of Contents

1: A Wedding of Inconvenience

It was almost sunset, the end of the Moon's two-week long Day. Spherical spaceships from eight planets cast long shadows across the flat expanse of Sinus Amoris Field. The Earth was at half-phase, vibrantly blue and white over the gray landscape. A long line of Moon Men in smooth, rotund, hard-shelled space suits waited on the road at the east side of the field.

"I realize this is kind of a weird question to ask on, you know, a business trip, but how do you people have sex?" Helene Friedman said.

"Every visitor asks that," Tom Easterday said, grinning. "The answer is, we rent a hotel room."

Helene looked around slowly, and finally said, "There are a couple of buildings for the port, but you said you live over on this side. I don't see any hotels or buildings. Just sun shades."

"Well, not here. We go to a hotel in air town."

"Air town?"

"That's what we call the crater cities, like Theophrastus, where you're staying. What hotel are you in?"

"The Hacienda," she said.

"Okay. Down at the end of that block, there's a hotel called the Caravansary. They cater to the Moon Men trade. For one thing, they have big doors, right? So we can get in and out wearing our tin cans." He smiled and waved at the line. The adult Moon Men wore hard-shell space suits with sliding ring joints at the knees and elbows. Each suit was backed with a huge boxy "backpack" holding life-support equipment, causing the wearers to stand bent forward in a simian posture. There were also some smaller suits for children, and a few pressurized "baby balls" propelled over the dusty ground by crawling toddlers, watched over carefully by their parents. Every suit was painted to express its owner's individuality: abstract stripes and curlicues (and one in polka dots!), manly scenes of eagles in flight or massive Aztec warriors carrying maidens, feminine themes of quaint Christmas cottages in the European woods, or flowers, or tropical fish.

Their helmets were large clear bubbles. The glass on the side of the setting sun was polarized to shade them from the blinding light. The polarization moved as they turned to talk to each other.

Helene's spacesuit was startlingly different. It was sewn of white fabric, the seams plainly visible. Her helmet was fitted close to her head and opaque except for a hinged glass faceplate. The suit wrinkled when she moved, and she carried exposed air bottles on her back. She appeared antique, out of place, strange. She looked like a visitor from another planet, as of course she was. The adults were polite, but children who came by stared at her.

Tom's suit was white, decorated with images that showed an unfashionable style even among the famously socially inept Moon Men: he had images of various spice plants, because he ran a business importing spices from Earth. The design was his own idea.

"What are we waiting for?" Helene asked Tom. Her suit had not been originally designed to communicate on the network the Moon Men used. Tom had found her a little transponder that sat on the shoulder of her suit like a parrot sitting on a pirate. Because she was facing toward Tom and had been talking with him, her radio signal went out with a network address that let only Tom hear her.

"We're going to be stepping off in just a moment," Tom said. "They usually time the wedding parade so that we'll reach the church exactly at sunset, which is kind of a big deal for us. There's sort of a tradition that we're active and rational and hustling during the Day, and romantic and meditative during the Night. Sunset is the best time to get married."

"I thought you worked around the clock at the field."

"Well, of course we do. I didn't say it was a real consistent tradition."

"Well, thank you for inviting me to this. I don't guess too many outsiders get to see a wedding in your ..."

"Village. Yeah, it's not a secret but we don't get a lot of tourists here either. I figured it would tell you something about us," Tom said, and added tactlessly, "I didn't have a date anyway."

A couple was working their way down the line, chatting with everyone in turn. The man was painted in a design suggesting a tuxedo, and the woman's suit was decorated in a very fetching design of antique pink roses on a linen background. Both of them had an odd oval patch of what seemed to be brown paper pasted on their suits over the heart area. "Hey, Tom!" the man said. The network control system evaluated

3

the situation, decided that Helene and Tom had enough proximity to be considered together, and adjusted the network address of his transmission so that Helene was included in the conversation.

"Hey, Gregor," Tom said. "Helene, meet the bride and groom. This is Gregor, who's an old college friend of mine, and his beautiful bride is Yeni. Nobody knows what she sees in him. Gregor, Yeni, this is Helene Friedman."

"Helene! We're so glad you're here!" Yeni said graciously, stepping forward to grasp both of Helene's hands. "Pay no attention to Tom, he's a goofball. Men don't understand weddings, anyway."

"It's true," Gregor said, grinning and mugging. "I have no idea what I'm doing. What am I doing? I don't understand this."

"Are you a friend of Tom's?" Yeni asked.

Helene said, "Actually, I'm a salesman. I'm here representing some agricultural producers from ... well, on Earth, and Tom's a customer. I need to talk him into buying more spices from us. He was nice enough to invite me here. I hope you don't mind. I don't know if Tom had RSVP'd for me or anything."

"Honey, it's the Moon," Yeni said, waving at the gray emptiness of the lunar landscape. "Two things we always have lots of, are room and food. You're as welcome as you can be. Did you know Tom has been involved in all the food for our reception? He brought in spices I've never even heard of. It's going to be so great, you'll love the food."

"Oh," said Helene.

"Oh," said Tom. "Um ... actually, Helene can't eat anything. Her suit's not equipped for it."

4

"You can't eat?" Yeni said.

"Helene," Gregor said, suddenly concerned, "that thing's got a limited air supply, too, right? How long have you got?"

"Another three hours."

"Tom, you get her back to air town with plenty of time to spare, okay? We don't want any drama at our wedding."

"No problem," Tom said.

Helene looked at their faces. "Don't you people have facilities to ... I don't know, get fresh air tanks or something?"

"We have algae," Yeni said. "There's like a couple of hundred meters of little clear tubes folded up in the life-support thing here, with lights and nutrients, and they throw off all the oxygen we need."

There was a sudden loud whistle sound, broadcast over the network with an address that let everyone in the wedding party hear it.

"That's the wedding planner!" Yeni cried. "We've got to go. I love her to pieces but she's a dictator! We'll see you at the reception!" They left, running up toward the front of the line with the long leaping steps of one-sixth gravity.

Everyone in the line straightened up and faced toward Sinus Amoris Village, a forest of sun shades. The band hired for the wedding stepped to one side of the line and began to play.

A Moon Man band was limited to instruments that could be played in vacuum. The ensemble had a lead electric guitarist, a bass player and a fiddler, all the instruments transmitting their signals by radio to the network controller. The keyboardist had an enormous vest that fitted over his space suit, holding keys that he played like a fat man fingering his waistcoat buttons. The drummer tapped with his fingers on various electronic keys and devices attached to the thighs and belly of his suit. The band also had a strong-lunged whistler who could contribute to the melody and stay on pitch, a skill much admired among Moon Men.

The band launched into a lively march and the wedding parade stepped off down the "street," a straight path into the village that was no different from the gray ground on either side except that it was delineated by lines of little lights.

At the van, the bride, the groom and the wedding attendants danced the whole way. The others danced, skipped or walked as they pleased or as they could. Little kids took advantage of the chance to run loops around the old folks. Tom tried a few dance steps but decided not to show up Helene, who could manage no better than a hobbled walk in her Earth-made suit.

"Where are we going?" Helene asked.

"First Baptist Church," Tom said. "It's on the village square, in the middle. Four blocks, about."

A wedding parade was an occasion in the village. Moon Men families lined the path with the children in the front, staying carefully on their side of the curb lights while the marchers kept to the street. The network set the addresses of their voices, the band's music and the marchers so that everyone could hear each other. The people called out, the marchers waved back with cheerful greetings and the band switched to a swing tune.

The village was a tent city of sun shades over empty, unpaved ground. Some shades were enormous sails or flat panels, and some were artistic arrangements of catenary curves between poles set at various angles. All of the shades were flexible solar power fabric and had spent the previous two weeks of Day charging underground batteries and capacitors. Now, as the sun touched the horizon, they began folding up automatically. Some were lowered to the ground and rolled up, others slumped into folds. As the shadows of the marchers grew longer and longer, the village was transformed.

What it was transformed into, was a barren expanse of moon dust no different from a million square kilometers around it, except for the folded sunshades, and the lines of little lights that marked off streets and individual lots of real estate. Some of the wall-less "houses" had tables and a few scattered cabinets, others not even that much. Helene looked past the people lining the parade route in wonder.

"Talk about a town where they roll up the sidewalks!" Helene remarked. "Does the town go away every Night like this?"

"Sure," Tom said. "We don't need any structures at Night. It's not like there's rain in the weather forecast, right?"

"What about little meteors or something?"

"That doesn't happen very often."

The sun set.

At the same instant that the last bit of sun slipped below the horizon, the glare vanished from the sky and all the glory of the stars sprang forth.

Each Moon Man's helmet depolarized to completely open a view of the Night sky. No sky on Earth, however clear and dark, could compare. The Milky Way was as thick as whipped cream, and stars down to tenth magnitude crowded each other almost to touching. The Earth was blue and white and lovable.

Helene gasped, looking up, and most of the Moon Men looked up as well, not blasé about the spectacle despite having seen it once a month all their lives. "Oh, my God!" Helene said. "You don't see this from ... you don't see this in town. Or on Earth, at least not where I live. This is ... "

"Glorious," Tom said. "I've got to tell you, you *never* get tired of it. There's an old joke – we're so lucky to live on skyfront property." Helene giggled, her head still bent uncomfortably back to allow her to look upward despite her confining helmet.

The wedding party danced, walked and (for the toddlers) rolled into the village square and entered the church, another square of empty ground marked off by lights.

They filed into lines organized by the ushers and sat on the ground, the groom's family on one side, the bride's family on the other. An usher, his uniform for the day an artificial flower boutonniere on his shoulder, pointed Tom and Helene into one line. Tom sat on the ground, an obviously well-practiced maneuver requiring a precise sense of balance.

Helene squatted tentatively and almost pitched forward. She stumbled back upright, barely avoiding bumping into the people seated in the line behind her, and was steadied by the usher. "Tom," she said, "I don't think I can sit down like that. My suit's not built for it."

"I should have thought of that! Sorry!" Tom said. "Come on, let's stand in the back." He rose up smoothly despite the weight and imbalance of his "backpack," and led Helene carefully through the lines of seated Moon Men to a position near the line of lights that marked the side of the church.

Helene stepped over the line to get a better view of the pulpit, and Tom grabbed her hand and pulled her back. "Don't stand over there," he said.

"It's an empty lot," she protested.

"It's ..." Tom glanced at the inner surface of his helmet and muttered something Helene could not make out. In the dark, she could see that the helmet was a computer display. Lines of glowing text ran up it. "It's the office of Selene Freight Forwarding," he said.

"Nobody's there right now. In fact, *nothing* is there."

"We just don't do that, okay? Look, they're starting."

The bridesmaids stood in a line on the left, all "dressed" in patterns of shimmering blue. Helene noticed for the first time that many of them had little oval-rimmed pictures or designs over the heart which were not part of the "bridesmaid dresses." The others had a blank white spot in that position, as did Tom.

The groomsmen lined up on the other side, all dressed in the tuxedo pattern. The minister wore a plain white space suit with a design suggesting a clerical collar around the base of the helmet.

There was also an adorable little girl, just big enough to have graduated from a baby ball to a miniature but complete Moon Man suit, standing to one side. She was not the ring bearer because the ceremony did not involve a ring. She was not a flower girl because the ceremony did not involve flowers. However, the custom of having cute little children in the wedding party was so ingrained that it was unthinkable to get married without at least one or two.

The band played Mendelssohn's wedding march and Gregor and Yeni paced slowly up the center aisle. The people turned their heads as they passed but did not shift: it wasn't practical when seated on the ground.

The wedding planner stood at the back near Tom and Helene. She had temporary control over the sound in every Moon suit in the church, and adjusted the distribution so that everyone could hear the music, the minister, the happy couple and the bride's mother bawling from the front row. When the minister began to speak, the bride's mother cried even louder but the wedding planner dialed down her volume.

Helene watched the ceremony and the other attendees, and out of the corner of her eye, noted that Tom was watching her face.

The minister stepped forward to deliver a pleasant and utterly predictable homily, inevitably based on Matthew 19:4-6. After a few minutes, Helene whispered to Tom, "How do the women put on all that makeup? They're exquisite. If I tried to use that much makeup, I'd be a total mess."

"There are little manipulators at various places in the suit," Tom whispered back. As Helene looked, two small, thin robot arms popped up inside his helmet. "You control them with touch pads in the gloves. It's how we put on makeup and cut our hair and do the man-grooming stuff you don't actually want me to talk about."

"Oh," Helene whispered, then added, "Why am I whispering? Why are *you* whispering?"

"When you whisper, the network understands you only want to talk to the person next to you, but also hear what's going on around you."

"What if I need to have everybody hear me, like if there's a fire?"

"Just raise your voice. The network will send your signal farther the louder you yell. But ... a *fire?*"

"You know what I mean. Hush up, the preacher's almost finished."

Gregor and Yeni spoke their vows to each other, and, kissing being impractical in a space suit, held hands. After a moment, they faced the audience together and peeled off the brown stickers from over their hearts, revealing the shared symbol they had chosen to represent their marriage to others. It was a stylized representation of the constellation of Libra, The Scales. They recited a little speech, alternating lines, about how they balanced each other, would always keep each other level, would survive the jolts of life and return to equilibrium, and other even sappier sentiments.

The audience went moderately crazy with applause, both mothers wailed, and the wedding planner let everyone hear them all.

Inasmuch as the First Baptist Church was just a bare rectangle of moonscape, with no features except the folded-up sunshades and some cabinets to hold supplies such as communion wafers and wine, there was no need for the wedding party to go anywhere. The band launched into a dance tune and the reception began.

The Moon Men stood and moved to the perimeter, not stepping over the line of lights, to open a dance floor in the middle. At one side, the groomsmen clustered around Gregor. On the other side, Yeni was surrounded by the bridesmaids. At a signal, they grabbed each of them by the ankles and tossed them high into the Night sky toward each other. Gregor and Yeni caught each other at the apogee by both hands and spun around as they fell slowly back to the ground under the pull of the Moon's mild gravity. They touched down with their feet close, leaned back still spinning and "gave weight", then opened up holding one hand and started their dance. Moon Men dances were limited to moves that could be done within the constraints of the ring gaskets of their space suits, and could not allow bending backward enough for the dancer to be toppled over by his backpack. Gregor and Yeni danced with high-kneed kicks and fancy footwork, couple spins and individual twirls, and lots of smoldering glances between them.

Gregor danced with his mother, Yeni with her father, the little girls of the families with each other. In a few moments everyone was dancing, except Tom and Helene.

"I don't think I can do this," Helene said.

"It's okay, everybody understands about your suit."

"The company bought me this suit. It was supposed to be a good one."

"Well, *sure*," Tom said. "If I wanted to buy a space suit, that's the *first* place I'd go shopping, is a factory at the bottom of the atmosphere where the only vacuum they ever experience is between the walls of their insulated coffee cups."

"All right, smart alec," Helene said. "If you ever come to Earth I'll take you swimming. I'll bet you'll be a natural."

The caterers arrived, pushing food-prep carts. Each cart had four big wheels suitable for rolling on Moon dust, a refrigerated locker for raw food, and a hot cook-top for frying. Each cart was covered by a big pressurized glass dome. The cooks set up around the perimeter.

Each cook inserted the arms of his suit through gasketed ports into the air space. When the dome was sealed, they could remove their gloves to have dexterity for cooking. In a trice, they were frying shrimp and diced chicken, chopping vegetables, toasting bread and seasoning the food with spices and sauces. Some of the Moon Men gave up dancing and came over to watch the process and chat.

"Tom," Helene said, "why are all those teenage boys around that one cart? Is that pizza or something?"

"The cook is Maria Fuertes," Tom said. "She's a good cook, but mainly she's a pretty young woman and the boys want to watch her bare hands moving. I think the boys' parents are going to break that up

13

pretty soon." Even as he spoke, one Moon Man woman stepped over and dragged one of the boys away by the elbow. The boy turned to a young girl and clearly asked her to dance. Even Helene could see the girl's nose go up: the boy left to try someone else.

One caterer served all the food. The others loaded their cooked foods into sealed transfer cans and delivered them to the server. The server had a rack of cylinders, about three fingers thick and as long as a hot dog. He loaded each cylinder with six round packets of different foods, each the size of a meat ball, and passed the cylinder through a little airlock to one of the waiting Moon Men.

The Moon Man would attach the cylinder to a fitting above the neck line of his suit and twist it sealed. Turning a knob at the end delivered a hot bite of food to his mouth.

Other caterers had drinks, supplied in a separate cylinder that attached to the other side of the suit. Helene said, "Tom, could I get a beer here?"

Tom looked embarrassed. "Um, you can get a Moon Man beer. I don't know if you've heard about our beer. We like it, but everybody else makes fun of it."

"Why? What's wrong with it?"

"It's flat," Tom said. "We don't drink carbonated beverages – there are a lot of problems in one-sixth gravity. Otherwise, it's pretty good beer."

"Now that I think about it," Helene said, "I don't have a way to drink your beer anyway. Forget I said anything."

"I'm really sorry," Tom said. "I didn't mean to make you feel conspicuous here. I guess I just wasn't thinking when I invited you."

"Don't worry about it, my suit has water," she said.

One of the women came over and pulled Tom into the dance. The fiddler was leading a lively tune and Tom danced a rustic, elbows-out clog step. A half-dozen women danced with him and passed him on to another.

One partner came up to Helene and introduced herself. "Hi, I'm Carmela. Tom said you're Helene, right?"

"Yeah. Hi, Carmela. Tom is sure dancing up a storm out there," she said.

"Tom's a popular guy," Carmela said. "You know, because of the food."

"I'm a salesman," Helene said. "I'm representing a bunch of Earth companies that sell food on the Moon, including Tom's company."

"The thing about Moon Men," Carmela said, "is that we totally love food. Tom's a terrific cook, which makes him a big ladies' man around here."

"I can see that," Helene said. "He told me he invited me to this wedding because he didn't have a date."

"Oh, hell, Tom could have brought any of a dozen women, including me, I guess. But if he picked any one of us, all the rest of us would have zinged him. I think you're sort of a safety date."

"Glad I could help," Helene said flatly.

"Do you want to dance?" Carmela said.

15

"I couldn't dance like that even back on Earth," Helene said. "Much less wearing this sausage casing. How do you do it?"

"Oh, these suits move better than yours, and anyway, we grow up in them. Come on, we can figure out some things you should be able to do. It's a wedding, you're supposed to have a good time." She led Helene to the margin of the church and stepped over one of the lines to the outside.

"Are we supposed to be here?" Helene asked. "I got yelled at for doing this."

"Where did you go?" Helene pointed, and Carmela said, "Well, that's somebody's office. You can't just barge in. But we're in the street here, so it's okay. Now try stamping your feet."

Helene stamped one foot. In one-sixth gravity, she bounded up a meter before slowly returning to the ground. "Okay," Carmela said. "So that's what *not* to do. The idea is to move your feet fast but light, so you don't leave the ground unless that's what you're trying to do, okay? Can you touch the ground heel-and-toe?"

"Um, no," Helene said. "I mean, I try, but I can't bend my ankle that much."

"Try moving one foot side to side. Okay, that's good. Now back and forth, flat to the ground. Now one leg, then the other leg. Good! Left back, left out, right back, right in. You're getting it!"

Some other women stepped "outside" to join them in the street. One of them stood behind Helene and said, "Helene? It is Helene, right? It's strange not to know somebody's name. Look, I'll be behind you and I'll catch you before you can fall, so don't worry about it. You kick up your legs the best you can."

Gradually Helene achieved a clumsy box step that was fast enough to stay in time with the music. The women hovered protectively over her. One woman who tried to help, though, actually did fall backward and had to be caught by two of the others.

"I'm sorry!" Helene said. "Did I knock into her or something?"

"That's Susanna," Carmela said, whispering. "Nice lady, friend of mine, but she's kind of a drunk. I've been at weddings before with her."

"Oh," Helene said. "I'm kind of surprised you people ever get drunk. I mean, you're so careful about everything."

"If her blood alcohol goes over 0.06, her suit will automatically give her a shot of sober-up," Carmela said. "She's at 0.03 now. She'll be all right."

"You know what her blood alcohol level is?"

"Oh, right, you're new here. Helene, Moon Men have no secrets. As long as we talk to each other every so often, the network figures we know each other, and I can see ... well, whatever the suit knows. Blood alcohol level, temperature, weight, how much she's been eating. Actually, looking at Susanna's blood sugar, if she would just eat some food along with slugging down all that wine, she'd be okay."

"You don't have any privacy at all!" Helene said.

"Not a bit," Carmela said cheerfully. "You do, of course. You know, when we go into air town we meet up with strangers, but out here in the village it's really kind of odd to stand next to somebody who's a complete mystery. You think maybe Tom likes the woman-of-mystery thing?"

"I'm here on business."

"So you are. Okay, ready to dance? Here comes Tom now, but he's too late! Sorry, Tom, the lady's taken!"

"I'm woofed anyway," Tom said. There was perspiration on his face, and little manipulators reached up from the trunk of his suit to wipe his forehead. He stood with his feet slightly wide and his suit stiffened into the "at rest" position. "Helene, you sure you want to try this?"

"It's a wedding. I'm supposed to have fun."

"Then go to it, lady. I'll just watch."

Carmela led Helene back across the border into the church, and out on the dance floor. The band seemed tireless, and nearly all the guests who were not clustered around the food carts and open bar were still dancing. The fiddler was still leading them in country tunes, and in a moment Helene was part of a group of three women and one man making a rough circle, all dancing for each other.

She stepped back and forth, occasionally making a misstep that sent her up from the ground. Grinning, Helene moved faster, trying to stay up with the others. She lifted her arms and twirled around, bowed at the waist, waved her hands. Sweat dotted her face and misted her faceplate, and the others cheered and urged her on.

Helene stumbled and fell to her knees. She looked down in horror as seams pulled open on both legs. Puffs of air escaped her suit and turned to steam which almost instantly vanished in the vacuum.

Helene screamed.

2: Town and Country

Working like a precision-trained team, which in fact any two Moon Men chosen at random were, the man and woman on either side of Helene reached their arms behind them to pop open a compartment in their backpacks, pulled out rolls of tape and ran to her. They pulled her up by the arms. Helene's eyes were wild as she looked from one to the other. In moments, they wrapped tape around both legs of her suit. Another woman had pulled an instrument out of another backpack compartment and ran it over every part of Helene's space suit. She detected a tiny leak in one elbow and they taped that as well. Other dancers crowded around to offer Helene words of comfort, but the original three spoke not at all until their repairs were done.

"Helene, it's okay!" Carmela said urgently. "You're tight now! Relax, breathe, it's okay."

Tom came bounding over at the same moment the band realized what was happening and stopped playing. "Tom, I ..." Helene said, and could go no further, gasping and swallowing.

"God almighty," Tom said. "What the hell kind of engineers do you have on Earth? This suit is a piece of crap! You're trusting your life to something made on a sewing machine?"

The bride and groom ran to them, and Yeni put a hand on Helene's shoulder, a gesture that was not common for Moon Men. After a moment, Yeni stepped back and raised her voice to address everyone.

"This is my wedding day," Yeni said. "We are *not* going to have bad stories about my wedding day. Gregor, honey, we've got to get this woman a decent suit. Can we set up a fund?"

"I'm on it," Gregor said. "Give me a minute, I'll set up a bank account."

"Everybody," Yeni said, "will you help us turn this around? We'll get her back to air town, but then poor Helene couldn't ever come back here without a new suit. Gregor and I will put in ... I don't know, forty sequins? Are we okay with that, babe? ... Okay, we'll put in forty. We haven't bought suits in my family in years. What does a Moon suit go for these days?"

"About five hundred fifty," somebody called out. "You two don't need to put in that much."

"Gregor, you got that donation account?" someone else asked.

"Here you go," Gregor said. Helene looked from one to another as text scrolled up the inner surfaces of everyone's helmets except hers.

"Helene, I got you into this," Tom said. "I'm in for fifty sequins."

Voices from the crowd added "Twenty," "Fifteen," "Twenty-five."

In three minutes Yeni said, "Made it! Thank you all, I love you folks! Tom, will you get this woman into town before something else busts? Helene, we're going to get you a real Moon Man suit. Nobody on Earth knows how to make the suits we live in. I mean, *seams*? Honest to God, what were they thinking?"

20

"Thank you! This is ..." Helene said, crying again.

"Honey, it's okay. We're glad to do it. You come back when you're dressed decently."

"Is this wedding still going to be going on?" Helene managed to ask.

"No," Yeni said. "Even Moon Men can't party that long."

"Sure we can!" somebody yelled. "I didn't get in on the suit, so beer for everybody!"

"Yang, *we're* paying for the beer," Gregor said.

"That's why everybody can have another one!"

"Tom, get going," Yeni said. "Helene, we're going into town for our honeymoon starting tonight, so maybe we'll see you there, okay? You just don't move your legs and arms more than you have to, and Tom'll get you set up. Everybody, give Helene a send-off!" Everyone cheered and waved goodbye. The music started up again as they walked away.

The monorail station was on Sinus Amoris Field, at the pressurized passenger terminal building. Tom led Helene out of the village, carefully walking only on the designated streets until they stepped onto the field. Once there, he headed diagonally across the various landing pads, which were also nothing but bare ground marked off into large squares. A spherical spaceship was coming down on the far side of the field, cradled in a tugboat frame piloted by a Moon Man.

"That was really nice of them, to kick in for a suit," Helene finally said. "I thought I was going to die."

"Well," Tom said, looking at her, "with that tight suit you're wearing, probably the worst that would have happened would be some big, sore, red strawberry marks on your legs. But I'm sure we got to you in time to prevent that. You should be fine." Helen was walking like a clumsy crab, trying not to bend her knees. She sashayed back and forth, trying to keep up.

"This place is so scary," she said. "How do you live, knowing everything in the environment is trying to kill you?"

"Everything?" Tom said, grinning. "Helene, there's *nothing* here. Vacuum is nothing, and all this Moon dust is not nothing but it isn't worth much, either. Nothing is scary. I guess I mean that nothing *isn't* scary." He continued, "Tourists always think there must be some beautiful scenery on the Moon, but the truth is it's all dusty flat ground or rounded hills, pretty much the same everywhere. Our environment is each other."

"I sort of thought you must have a bunch of special words for different kinds of Moon dust."

"Like that thing where the Eskimos are supposed to have a lot of words for snow? Nah. We just call it 'dust' if we talk about it at all, which we hardly ever do. By the way, that's another advantage of getting an actual Moon suit – the dust won't stick to it. You're filthy from trying to dance in that fabric suit."

"It'll be good to get back into town. I'm going to hit the hotel and take a shower," Helene sighed.

They walked up to the passenger terminal, with the monorail overhead disappearing into an airlock above their heads. To Helene's surprise, Tom led her around the building to the back. There was a Moon Man attendant there, crouched down to work on some machinery. The backpack of his suit was decorated with a brightly-colored cartoon of a popular local band, all depicted in their Moon suits as well.

"Hey, Jimbo," Tom said. "Get us a rack to town, okay?"

"Hi, Tom," the man said, standing and turning. He looked askance at Helene.

"She's from Earth," Tom explained.

"Hi, Miss," Jimbo said. "Aren't you going to want to go inside and ride in the car?"

"Oh, we're going to get her a Moon suit and then she'll be one of the gang," Tom said. "Helene, I know you rode the pressurized car out here from town, but let's go back Moon Man style. This is cool, trust me."

"Jimbo," Helene said, smiling, "Tom's kind of ... you know. If he says it's cool, should I believe him?"

Jimbo bowed, with a smile. "Yeah, you're coming to know our Tom. But it'll be okay. I'm pretty sure you'll like it."

"Well, thank you."

They waited a moment while Jimbo disappeared into a storage shed. "Tom," Helene said, "do you know everybody in the village?"

"Sinus Amoris village is only about a thousand people," Tom said. "This is a fairly small landing field. Of those, I guess I've met everybody who's on my shift, which would be about a third of that. We have to work around the clock, so everybody is on a

23

particular shift. My family works first shift, midnight to eight Greenwich time, along with Jimbo here."

"I didn't think of that," Helene said. "What time of day is it for you?"

"Evening," Tom said. "I'm okay. I wouldn't usually sleep for a couple of hours yet. Ah, here comes our rack."

Jimbo returned pulling a metal frame like a two-seat ski lift, suspended a meter off the ground by two cables from a small bogie mounted on the monorail. Tom asked "Ready?" and while Helene was still considering her answer, lifted her up and put her into one of the seats. Jimbo held the frame steady, then reached across her lap and tightened a seat belt around her. Tom climbed aboard and fastened himself in.

"Get going," Jimbo said. "The shuttle to town leaves in about a minute."

"Okay, and thanks, Jimbo!" Tom said. He touched a control on the armrest and the bogie began to move.

"You two have a good time!" Jimbo called.

"She's here on a business trip!" Tom yelled back. The bogie accelerated smoothly, floating on superconducting magnets a little distance above the rail, and they lifted and headed toward Theophrastus Crater.

Behind them, the airlock opened and the pressurized car holding travelers from eight planets left the terminal and followed them. Helene could just barely turn back to look at them. She saw faces staring at them out of the front window.

"I didn't see anybody riding like this when I came out from town," she said, yelling as though she needed to shout over the noise of wind. When she realized the ride was silent, she lowered her voice.

"This is how we always to go town," Tom said. "We take up a lot of space if we get in the gondola with the regular passengers, so we do it this way."

"Why do they let you?"

"Moon Men run the monorail. Moon Men run *everything* outside of town except the spaceships, and the spaceships couldn't go if we didn't load them and fix them up and all."

Helene said "Whee!" as the rail turned. Their feet swung outward. She found herself looking up at the thickly spattered stars, and as they straightened up, looking down at the dark ground zipping by below them. Their Earth-light shadows scampered over the hills and craters of the moonscape.

The rail joined another line coming from the east. Their rack sailed over the junction and they were riding just behind an unmanned cargo pod. "That's from Mare Crisium," Tom remarked, pointing to it. The cargo pod sped up a little on its linear induction motor to keep a distance from them. "They're shipping aluminum nuggets to a factory outside town, that forms them up to be exported to Earth. The company is run by air-towners but the actual work is done outside by Moon Men."

"How do you know that?" Helene asked. "I don't see any markings." Tom pointed a finger to the text scrolling across his helmet just below his eye level, and Helene said, "Oh, yeah." The cargo pod was swinging a little after making its turns, and Tom and Helene were swinging as well on a different, faster rhythm. Looking at the cargo pod made her a little queasy, so Helene looked up at the stars until the rack stopped rocking.

"This is nothing like riding in the gondola," Helene remarked. "When I came out I was the only one in a spacesuit. I had my faceplate up, and I was chatting with a couple from Nova Terra and we were drinking coffee. The windows were all darkened because, you know, it was Day. They were going to visit their kids on a planet called Amity."

"It's fun to ride the monorail during the Day, too," Tom said. "But yeah, it's prettier at Night. Tourists never really see much of the Moon, and they don't see us — you know, Moon Men — at all. They stay in the air, we're outside. A lot of people don't even know we're here. I guess they think the work all gets done by elves or something."

"Tom," Helene said hesitantly, "I'm new here and nobody on Earth knows much about you either. The company sent me to you because you buy spices through us. What do Moon Men do, anyway?"

"There are eight planets in the Ecumene, and every path between one and the other involves a layover here on the Moon. We're stevedores and longshoremen and ship's chandlers at the field, and mechanics and factory workers everywhere else. We do all the work that has to get done outside of the pressurized cities and buildings. I mean, we're nobody special. Mostly we're employees of companies that have offices in the air towns. But we've got some things people in air town never see.

Honest, Helene, look up at the sky. Isn't this something you're glad you could do?"

"It's glorious," Helene said, and was rapt and silent for a long while. Eventually she said, "But you own your own business, right?"

"Yeah, and I'm a real titan of industry. I have two employees. They're both part-time, high-school kids. Actually, I'm kind of unusual because I rent a pressurized building out by the field. You can't handle spices in vacuum, they dry out and taste bad."

"Couldn't the Moon Men have their own pressurized buildings out by the port, and come inside at the end of the day?"

"We like it this way," Tom said. "Besides, getting in and out of these suits is kind of a process. You need a technician to get out of a Moon suit, and then more help getting back in. It's easier just to stay suited up. Look, we're coming into town. This is a pretty good view, too."

Theophrastus Crater was a ring wall of rock nine kilometers across, topped by a low dome of clear plastic stabilized by a web of titanium cables. The dome was twelve meters thick and filled with water that harbored algae to supply food and oxygen to the city. During the Day it basked in the sunlight, but at Night it was lit by lamps from below. It bulged up like a cabochon emerald, glowing green and alive in contrast to the dead gray of the lunar landscape around it, beautiful and defiant against the vacuum and cold stars.

The rail split in several directions. The cargo pod was switched one way, they were sent another and when Helene looked back, she could see that the passenger gondola had been sent to yet a different destination.

The rail rose up, and they were delivered silently and swiftly to an open door where the rim of the crater met the dome. The rack braked to a stop inside a metal-walled room decorated with safety posters Helene did not have time to read, as well as a big pressure gauge mounted on the wall. An airlock door slid shut behind them. Tom said, "This gate is just for Moon Men. We don't have to go through all of the checks tourists go through." He unbuckled and jumped off, then helped Helene unclip her seat belt. They stood side by side until the air pressure reached normal.

However, the inner door did not open. A video display flicked on in front of them, showing a policeman in a yellow uniform. "Hello, Thomas Easterday," he said. "Who's your companion?"

"Helene Friedman of Earth," Tom said. "Sorry, I forgot you can't read her."

"Helene Friedman, please open your faceplate and face the camera. You are already registered in Theophrastus?"

"Yes, I am," Helene said. "The Hacienda Hotel."

"Got it," the policeman said. "Welcome to our city. In the future, we ask you to please use the regular passenger gate." The screen went dark and the inner door rolled up to show them the interior of the city.

"No problem," Tom said. "Once we get you a Moon suit, you'll be identified and you can go anywhere." Tom detached his helmet — a process of several steps — pulled it off and tucked it under one arm. Without it, his head looked foolishly small compared to the suit body. He had sandy blonde hair, cut short, and ordinary, pleasant features.

"I don't think I can get this helmet off by myself," Helene said. "The technician put it on."

Tom looked at it and said, "I don't want to guess how to do that. But can you open the faceplate?"

"I can." The faceplate was hinged at the top. Helene opened it, looking even sillier than Tom with the curved plastic over her head like an Easter bonnet. She breathed the air deeply. "Well, here we are," she said, as they entered the dome. "Breathing air. Together."

"Yeah," Tom said glumly. "Did you ever think that the air you're breathing in, was previously breathed out of the wet lungs of a couple of thousand other people in this dome?"

"That's how air works," Helene said lightly. "Come on, where is this Moon suit shop?"

"It's on Elm Street," Tom said. "It's not too far from this gate. Do you want to walk? Or should we call a cab?"

"A cab," Helene said definitely. "It's hard to walk in this rubber girdle."

Apparently Tom's helmet was still networked to his suit even when it was removed. He held it in front of him and studied the display scrolling up the inner surface, then said, "It'll be a couple of minutes. Cabs are all busy right now, for some reason."

Theophrastus City was a ring of low mountains around a plain that was fifty city blocks across, although about half of it was farmland. The dome that was so beautifully lit in the Night when seen from outside, was a dull green when seen from beneath.

The inner crater walls were built up with apartments holding the city's permanent residents, the flat roof of one dwelling serving as the patio of the house above. They also supported zig-zag streets, offices, schools and open-air cafes.

The flat crater floor served travelers who were waiting out layovers between ships. The biggest buildings were neon-flashing casinos and hotels. There were restaurants promising the cuisines of every planet of the Ecumene. Strip clubs, bars, brothels, sports arenas, music halls and every other kind of amusement all vied to separate tourists from their money.

"The sky looks like storm clouds," Helene said. "That's kind of depressing."

"Does it?" Tom said. "It's green. I thought storm clouds were gray? Anyway, it's a lot nicer during the Day. Doesn't seem to have stopped the bird-men, though." In one-sixth gravity, it was possible to strap on a pair of rental wings and fly under the dome, and the air was full of flying tourists. They fell out of the sky fairly often – a young woman in the air right in front them suddenly turned too sharply and fell, waving her wings wildly, down to the floor of the plaza. She landed on her shoulder without much injury, protected by the weak gravity, and a flight instructor stooped in response, holding his wings together over his head. The instructor fell relatively quickly, catching himself with a sudden snap of his wings two meters off the ground, and landed deftly beside his student.

"I haven't had the courage to try that yet," Helene said. "I suppose I should, while I'm here."

"I never have either," Tom said. "It always looked dangerous to me."

"Well, you can relax for a while," Helene said. "It's safe in here."

"I guess. Truth is, I get anxious while I'm around crowds ... I mean, crowds of people with their faces hanging out and ... that sounds neurotic, doesn't it? Anyway, I relax when I'm back out in vacuum. Depends on what you're used to, I suppose."

The cab arrived, an open car with four seats. Tom was obliged to sit in the back row because his suit took up more than one seat. He spoke into a microphone to enter their destination and the cab rolled silently down a sloping road to the city floor.

The car took them through plazas and streets crowded with travelers. In the unchanging pleasant weather of the domed crater, clothing was largely optional. Tourists strolled about in the national costumes of all the nations on all the planets. Helene took it all in with interest, but Tom looked uncomfortable and somewhat scandalized.

The men among the tourists wore costumes ranging from business suits (one-piece coveralls in sober dark colors, with a contrasting stripe down the pants legs) to blissfully unattractive vacation wear: shorts with or without a shirt, sandals, funny hats, togas, pajamas and in many cases complete nudity.

Some of the women were nude as well, while others sought comfort in prissy complete cover-ups − chadors, Mother Hubbard gowns, tailored suits, sack dresses. Most of them, however, appeared to be taking advantage of traveling to wear clothing that was sexier than good taste would allow back home.

They wore outfits which presented whatever portion of the anatomy was usually hidden in their culture. Their garments variously emphasized the breasts, buttocks, belly, face or legs of the wearer, to better or worse effect.

The Moon Men in the crowd wore their huge, brightly-decorated space suits with helmets off. Other people collided with their hard shells as they walked on the boulevards.

Elm Street, at the corner of Sixth Avenue, was lined with small shops offering clothing from all of the various worlds, for those who wanted the clothing of their home planets and those who specifically wanted something different. Tom led the way to a shop with an unusually wide and high door, marked "Sarro's Engineered Garments."

They were met by a stout, gray-haired woman in a summery long dress. She wore a wide device mounted on a wrist band and glanced at the display as they entered, then smiled and said, "Come on in, Tom."

"Hi, Oksana," Tom said. "How are you? Oksana, this is Helene Friedman. Helene, this is Oksana Sarros. My family's been buying suits at her store for a long time." Helene said hello.

She looked sharply at the tape holding Helene's suit together. "Dear," she said, "I'm so glad you're all right! You had a seam open? That suit is from Pressure Protection in New Jersey, isn't it?"

"Is it? I guess so," Helene said. "You recognize it?"

"I'm in the business. You are at least the third person we've had from Earth who has come to us to replace that model of suit, although I must say nobody else had a rupture while they were outside. That's horrible! Those suits must be cheap, because I can't imagine why else anybody would buy one. Probably somebody else picked that out for you, right?" Helene nodded.

"Do you really need a space suit?" Oksana continued. "I don't want you to think I don't want your business, but if you're going back to Earth, you won't need a pressure suit. Even if you're going on somewhere else, most places you won't need a suit."

"We're going to get her a Moon suit," Tom said. "Here's the account information to pay for it."

"A Moon suit?" Oksana asked.

"Yes," Tom said.

"Well, if that's what you want. Actually, we just fitted your little nephew Joseph with a larger suit last week," Oksana said. "But I don't think I've ever sold a Moon suit to somebody who didn't come in already wearing one."

"It is kind of unusual," Tom said.

"Helene, is this what you want?" Oksana asked.

"Um, what am I signing up for? I guess I do. They bought it for me because I can't wear this suit anymore."

"I promise that when you trade that one in, I will never let anybody wear it again. Okay dear, you come with me. It will take a while to get you fitted. You probably don't have a bank account on the Moon, do you?"

"No. Why would I need a bank account?"

"You can't wear a Moon suit without a bank account. I'll get you all set up. Welcome to the Moon!"

"I'll just wait here," Tom said.

"You will *not*," Oksana said with asperity. "You go away somewhere and we'll call you when Helene is dressed. Now shoo!"

Tom said, "Okay, okay. I'll go get a drink or something. Oksana, find her a nice suit, will you? If there's not enough money, I can chip in some more."

"Certainly," Oksana said. "Now out you go. Helene, come on into the back room." As Tom was leaving, she said to Helene, "Men! As if I couldn't figure out what he's hoping to see."

"All of those tourist women and their weird clothes," Helene said. "I guess he can see anything he wants to, sitting outside."

"Except you, dear," Oksana said. She closed the door behind them.

3: A Dinner of Food

A laser measuring booth extracted every possible measurement from Helene's nude body, while she turned awkwardly with her arms over her head. Oksana fussed over the controls of the booth and repeatedly asked her to turn one way and the other, frowning at the display. Finally she was satisfied.

A messenger robot from Helene's hotel showed up at the door of the shop, a squat rolling cart with an open basket of Helene's laundry on the top. Oksana let it in, and Helene came out of the booth to say, "Oh, for Pete's sake. I just asked them to send me one set of clothes. Now everybody in the city gets a look at my bra and dirty socks."

"It's more than that," Oksana said, opening a compartment in the robot's body. "They cleaned out your room, it looks like. If that's your only suitcase there, then I think they sent everything you have."

"Why would they do that?"

Oksana queried the robot, using her wrist device. "Honey," she said slowly, "you just got kicked out of the Hacienda for non-payment. You don't have a room there anymore."

"What? Why?"

"They didn't say. Is your credit card maxed out or something?"

"The company set up the room. I couldn't finance a cheeseburger on my own card."

"Well, why don't you get dressed in your clothes and you can call them. I've got some work to get your suit components pulled together anyway." Oksana bustled out to the other room. Helene took everything out of the robot, which trundled off on its own, and dressed herself in a white blouse and gray skirt from her remaining clean clothes. Finally she pulled out her phone and sat down to call the hotel. Then she called her company back on Earth, putting up with the irritating one and a quarter second speed-of-light delay while trying to have a conversation.

Oksana found her sitting with her shoulders slumping. "Helene," she said, "what's wrong?"

"I got fired. They canceled my hotel room and dropped me. I've still got my ticket back home, but not a damn thing else."

"Why?"

"Oh, I ... I made some mistakes last week," Helene said. "Oksana, I guess I'm not going to need that Moon suit."

"It's all paid for. The people at that wedding did all right by you, Helene. I set your account up with a bank in Eratosthenes City, and you've got enough money left over to pay for air, water, food and everything for the next couple of weeks. Why not call it your Moon vacation? I know most people on Earth can't afford to come here."

"Where am I going to sleep?"

"Oh, Moon Men just sit down on the ground wherever they want. Actually, they all sleep together, like a herd of horses or something. I've never heard of any Moon Man sleeping alone, and I think if you try it a bunch of them will come over to ask if you're all right. Probably you should ask Tom if you can sleep with him and his family."

"Sleep with him? I barely know the guy."

"Moon Man style, dear. Safe in your own suit. Believe me, nobody ever has better personal space than a Moon Man." Oksana sat down beside her and put her arm around Helene's shoulder. "Helene, I've never heard of anybody wearing a Moon suit who wasn't a Moon Man. I'm not one, but I've been doing business with them all my life. They're as stiff as wrenches, they're the nicest people in any world, they're as shy as birds and they are all, every single one, plain weird. I see them with their suits off and you can just tell they're fussing about people breathing on them. I mean seriously, they're as strange as can be, but you'll never meet anybody friendlier.

They'll take care of you and you can have an adventure you can talk about when you get back to Earth."

"Are you from Earth?" Helene asked. "Are you going back?"

"No, I came here from Terra Nova," Oksana said. "And I can't go back. Once you've lived on the Moon long enough, your heart's too weak to live in normal gravity again. It's okay, I like it here and I have family here. But you're young, you can play around a while before you have to go back to work."

"Yeah, I can play around a while," Helene said, and burst into tears. Oksana waited silently.

"I am a salesman," Helene finally said, rambling mostly to herself. "I can talk people into things. I can. I'm good at it. I came here to sell food and I *am* going to sell food whether I'm on the payroll or not. If I come in with some good orders, they'll have to take me back. If not, there are co-ops I can bring those orders to and they'll be glad to have me. I've still got a job, the damn company just doesn't know it yet."

"There you are! Why don't you go find Tom?" Oksana said. "I've got some suit parts being printed up for you – things that I didn't happen to have in the right size. You take an hour or so and when you get back, I'll have everything ready." She looked at her wrist and said after a moment, "He's in a park about two blocks that way."

"You can find where he is?"

"I can find any Moon Man. Helene, once you put on that suit, anybody on the whole Moon will know where you are and what you're doing. You just have to get used to that."

Helene stood up. She moved a little too fast and bounced slightly off the floor, but was able to catch herself after a moment. "Hey," she said, "this is the first time I've tried wearing high heels since I got here. My feet don't hurt. This place has some advantages!"

"It actually does," Oksana said, smiling. "You run along and get lunch or something."

Aside from the odd green sky and the constant feeling of instability from the low gravity, walking in Theophrastus Crater City seemed like walking on a boulevard on a nice spring day on Earth. The people, in their crazy mix of costumes, sauntered pleasantly without rushing. Street vendors with booths and pushcarts sold food ranging from hot dogs to pho. Helene passed two bookstalls, one dedicated to naughty books for tourists from more repressed cultures. Travel between planets required being in a ship that was removed from all electronic communication for four days, a terrifying prospect that fueled the sales of more physical books on the Moon than were sold on any individual planet.

Tom was sitting on the ground in a small park dominated by one hugely over-sized elm tree, which had given the street its name and grown high in the low gravity. Birds perched on some smaller branches, and human fliers rested on the larger branches. He was playing a game displayed in his glass helmet, which he held in front of him. He looked up when Helene arrived and smiled broadly. "Helene!" he said. "You look ... you look great. You've got long hair!" He rose smoothly to his feet.

"Hi, Tom. Thank you, I guess you haven't actually seen my hair before, have you? Why don't you sit on a bench or something?"

"The suit doesn't really fit on a bench for mouth breathers," Tom said. "Um, wait, I mean people without suits."

"'Mouth breathers,'" Helene said. "You've got your own little racist name for normal people. Nice."

"We are nice people, just not perfect," Tom said. "I just slipped, I shouldn't have said that."

"Some of your best friends are mouth breathers, right?"

"I'm sorry. Anyway, I wanted to say that I don't know much about hair – we all wear ours pretty short so it doesn't get in the way. Don't tell me this if I'm not supposed to ask, but is that your natural color? It's lovely."

"Mouse brown? Tom, *nobody* would purposely dye her hair this color. Of course it's the real me." Tom reached his hand tentatively up and Helene said, "Down, boy! It's not polite to touch a woman's hair – or anything – unless she says you can. However, if I ever do let you touch my hair, I guarantee it will be with your hands. Why don't you take off those gauntlets?"

"Oh. Sure, sure. I just didn't think of it." Tom detached his gloves and clipped them to holders on the thighs of his suit.

"I have to wait for my suit to be ready," Helene said. "I'm hungry. How about that restaurant there, that says 'Authentic Moon Man Cuisine'?"

"You don't want to go *there*," Tom said instantly. "That's just for tourists. Nobody understands Moon Man food except Moon Men."

"It's right here, other people are eating there, I'm hungry and I'll pay," Helene said. "You can tell me what's wrong with it while we're eating."

Tom allowed himself to be led through a little gate into the restaurant, which was an "outdoor" cafe. This restaurant apparently either did attract Moon Men or wanted to appear that they did. A hostess produced a huge chair designed to accommodate the backpack of a Moon suit, and led them to a table with a normal chair for Helene. Menus were displayed on the surface of the table.

"Well, let's try this one," Tom said, studying the listings.

"*A Chase Across Salted Textures to Savory*," Helene read. "What does that even mean? It's food, right? You're not going to make me eat poetry?"

"If they do it well, it's good food," Tom said. "It has chicken and usually a little shrimp, with different vegetables and some spiced applesauce at the end. It's a classic meal, but they'll probably mess it up." He touched the order button, sat back and added graciously, "It comes with a Moselle wine and cold mineral water. I don't know, maybe they won't screw it up."

"I'm sure you'll let me know if it doesn't measure up," Helene said. She looked around and waved at the other diners. "Everything comes in those little tubes?"

"The gray ones are called 'sixpacks' and hold the food. The white ones are bottles of drink. Real ones are made of metal, these are just plastic imitations. I suppose tourists don't know the difference."

A rolling robotic cart delivered four sixpacks and two tubes of drink to each of them, in an orderly arrangement on a plate. Tom bowed his head to say a brief grace, while Helene watched, then picked up the right-most sixpack. "Okay," he said, "start with this one. It has – I mean, assuming they did it right – a bland chicken meatball, two balls of green beans in a sharp sauce, then two spicy meatballs and finally some bread. You bring out the food one bite at a time by twisting the knob at the bottom."

"Do I get a fork or anything? Even a napkin?"

"No, and no. This is Moon Man 'six-bite cuisine', designed to be eaten in a helmet. Take each of the six bites in one gulp, chew and swallow and appreciate it a moment, then go to the next. Take the wine and mineral water when you want to. If you bite the food into two pieces or anything, it won't matter *here*, but if you were in your Moon suit you could get crumbs in your helmet. There's no good way to use a napkin so you don't get one, just don't get sloppy when you eat."

"You know, Tom," Helene said, "when you use the phrase 'six-bite cuisine' I can practically hear the little trademark symbol. I take it you eat everything in six bites?"

"Yes. Six bites to a pack, three sixpacks make a dinner. Go ahead, try it."

Helene held the sixpack up to her mouth, twisted the knob to expose a pale small meatball and popped it into her mouth. She was about to go on to

41

the next bite when she noticed Tom was still chewing. He swallowed and said, "Take your time. Food should be savored. I have to say, that one was done about right."

"It's okay, I guess," Helene said. "Why is it bland, and why do you want to 'savor' bland food?"

"To set you up for the next bite," Tom said. "Everything in a six-bite meal has a reason. It's like music or dancing. There's a logic to the sequence. Now the first green-bean ball."

Helene exposed the next bite, a wad of chopped green beans held together by a white sauce. She ate it and gasped. "Oh, my God. What is that?"

"Horseradish sauce. Tasting the bland meatball sets you up for that sensation. When you're ready, try the next green-bean bite. It's also horseradish, but less strong and with a little umami from meat broth, also some garlic and fat." Tom ate the next bite, then made a face. "Tarragon," he complained. "These guys don't know what they're doing. I understand tarragon on green beans but who puts tarragon on top of horseradish? Who puts *anything* on top of horseradish?"

"That was pretty good, though," Helene said, after swallowing it. "Better than the first one. How do you get that stuff to hold together in a ball?"

"We mix in some tasteless alginates to make adhesive sauces," Tom said. "That's something that nobody does but us – we have a whole range of sticky sauces to make things into bite-size balls. Yeah, that was actually tasty but it's just ... incoherent, you know? The cooks here don't understand food logic."

They ate the spicy meatballs, which were not hot with chilies but rather made savory with curry masalas, slightly different for each meatball. The bread was a warm, small roll with butter in the middle.

"This is our ethnic cuisine," Tom chattered away as they started the next sixpack. "We eat everything that comes bite-size – pierogi, sushi, gnocchi, bao, raviolis, little slider hamburgers held together with adhesive condiments. In our own way, we're just as quaint and ethnic as ... I'm not too up on Earth culture. Who's ethnic on Earth? Mexicans? Mongolians? Anyway, we're ethnic like them."

Finally Helene held up one hand and said, "Tom, I *sell* food. I don't have a romantic relationship with it. Shut up and eat, okay?"

She ate each bite precisely and conscientiously chewed and swallowed with consideration. Tom ate absently, looking at her. "Tom," she finally said, "why are you looking at me like that?"

"You're very pretty. Also, I'm trying to figure you out, I guess. You seem mysterious to me."

"I can imagine. You probably don't know any other women whose blood sugar level and current weight and muscle tension you can't read on your display, right?"

"Um, yeah. They say the eyes are windows to the soul, so I'm thinking ..."

"Well, stop gazing into my eyes!" Helene said. "It's creeping me out. My boobs are down here!" Tom blushed and looked away, and was silent for a while.

The last two bites were quivering balls of applesauce flavored with cinnamon and allspice.

Helene looked at the first one dubiously and asked, "What holds this together?"

"It's called 'spherification'," Tom said. "You drop spoonfuls of ...".

"I don't want to know," Helene said. She swallowed the ball, smiled and quickly ate the last one. "Tom, that was good. Thank you! Where do I pay?"

"It already came out of my bank account at the moment I placed the order. When you're wearing a Moon suit, you're always connected to your bank account. It's okay, thank you for having dinner with me. I'm sorry if I was rude."

"I'm sorry that I was rude, too. Let's go get my new suit. I've always wanted to know what I would look like wearing an oil drum." They stood and left the cafe.

"You'll look terrific," Tom said gallantly as they entered the crowd on the street.

"How do Moon Men guys feel about curvy women when all of your women, not to mention the men, have exactly the same shape?"

"Um," Tom said. There was a period of silence.

"Well put," Helene said.

Oksana led Helene into the back room of the shop, leaving Tom to page idly through a display of upgrade components on the wall. After a few minutes they returned. Helene lurched in, awkward in her new, plain white Moon suit.

"What is this thing made of?" she gasped. "It's heavy as lead!"

"Almost," Oksana said. "Actually, it's tungsten."

"Why didn't you just make it out of solid gold? If I'm going to haul around all this weight, I should get some flash, you know?"

"Tungsten provides better protection against radiation," Tom said seriously. "Your helmet is leaded glass for the same reason. Also, the suit meters out some anti-radiation drugs."

"I am quite aware that this suit has needles that plug into my arms, not to mention appliances plugged into my ... " Helene said. "No wonder you need a technician to get it on or off." She suddenly gasped, "I've got an itch! Oh, my God! I could die from this! How do I scratch my back?"

"Say, 'Suit, scratch my back'," Oksana said.

Helene said that without effect. Oksana said, "Speak into the helmet."

Helen tried that, and looked startled. "Suit, down a little. Suit, to the left. Suit, up. Okay. Yeah, that's it," she said, and sighed.

"You can give the suit a name if you'd rather not say 'Suit'," Tom said helpfully.

"This suit is not just all over me like a cheap suit, it's plugged in to ... um, places," Helene said. "I'm going to call it Ramone? Fifi? Robbie the Robot? Farfel the Wonder Dog? That's disturbing on so many levels. I'll stick with 'Suit', thank you. Oksana, is there a user manual for this monster?"

"Just ask the suit to do anything you need," Oksana said. "As you get used to each other, it will get better at figuring out what you want. There are also a bunch of training videos you can watch, although I've got to say most of them are aimed at little kids."

"You can also use 'quickspeak,'" Tom said. "It's a special control language."

"I wondered what everybody was mumbling around me."

"You don't have to use quickspeak, the suit will respond to anything you ask in normal language. It's just convenient," Tom said. "Also, see this little dimple on your arm?" He pointed, and Helene nodded. "That's an interface that connects to another interface on the tip of the second finger of everybody's left hand. If you can't figure out how to do something, let another Moon Man put his interface finger there and he can talk to your suit's controller directly."

"Ooh, sexy," Helene said. "I bet all the girls want you to touch them on the interface, tiger."

Oksana went back into the other room and returned with Helene's rolling suitcase. Tom looked at it and raised his eyebrows.

"I'd like to come visit your family, Tom," Helene said. "I have to make a bunch of sales calls to other Moon Men, so if you don't mind, let me stay in the village tonight."

"Sure, of course," Tom said. "But you won't need your suitcase."

"It's an Earth thing," Helene said, smiling tightly. "We like to have our stuff with us."

"Oh, okay. Moon Men don't really have 'stuff'."

"I've noticed."

"Do you have toothpaste or anything liquid in there?"

"Oops. I do!" Oksana had to open the suitcase for her since Helene could not do it with her gloves on. She and Helene went through the contents and discarded anything that would boil and burst in vacuum.

"Oksana, do you mind if I use your toilet before we go?" Tom asked.

"Of course not," Oksana said.

"Toilet!" Helene sputtered, suddenly appalled. "I just ... I just assumed I could just ..."

"Of course you can," Tom said. He walked to the corner of the room and opened a panel to reveal a sort of vending machine. He reached back and extracted a box from another compartment in his backpack, and inserted it in a receptacle. "Every few days, you pull this out and put it into a toilet. There are a bunch of them in the village. The toilet takes it and gives you a fresh cartridge." He retrieved the box and plugged it back into his backpack.

"What happens to the ... you know, the contents?"

"It gets sold to a broker and you get a little credit in the bank. Organics are always worth some money." Tom looked into his helmet and said, "You've only got about a one-eighth load right now. Don't worry about it."

"Suit," Helene said through unmoving lips, "don't let this guy see *any* of my information ever again."

"The suit won't take an order like that, honey," Oksana said. "Moon Men think it's a safety thing. Other people always get to see how you're feeling. All right, you're ready to go. You've got air and water and battery charge, and you've got money in the bank."

47

"What happens if I run out of money?"

"The village will cover you, at least enough to get back to the city here," Oksana said. "Nobody ever dies from being poor in the Moon Men. But you may have to transfer some funds in from Earth or make some money if you're going to stay longer than a week or two."

"You can stay a little longer than that just with what you've got," Tom said, looking again into his helmet. "I know some cheap sources."

"Stop looking at my bank account!" Helene said.

4: Helene Looks Nice

Helene rode the monorail rack uncomfortably, trying to hold her suitcase on her lap and ruefully realizing that Moon suits do not have a lap even when seated. She looked over at Tom on the seat next to her and asked, "Why don't these things have some kind of luggage space?"

"We don't carry luggage. The suit backpack has some storage space," Tom said. "Actually, we hardly ever carry anything in our hands. Look, there's another ship coming in to the field. I know the guy who's piloting that tug."

She looked down at Sinus Amoris Field a kilometer ahead of them, defined by rectangles of lights on the ground, then looked up into the glorious Night sky to see a flare of lights from the rocket engines of the tug, passing in front of the half-phase Earth. The tug was actually a huge open basket with rocket engines on the rim, and a belvedere on the side where the Moon Man harbor pilot stood. The spaceship sat in it like a soccer ball in a colander. The ship drifted gently down to the ground, gliding a little left and right as the pilot made corrections. "Why doesn't the pilot ride inside the ship?" she asked.

"Because it freaks out the passengers. We look weird to people from the planets, in our Moon suits," Tom said. "They always think the ship's in danger of being depressurized or something."

"You know, Tom, I'm not really 'us.' I'm just wearing the suit for a while."

"Sure, sure. But you've got to admit, it's a nicer suit than what you had."

"Yeah, it is. What will Oksana do with the old one?"

"Break it up for materials. We never waste anything around here if we can possibly avoid it. The only reason your new suit was as cheap as it was is that almost all of the parts came from old Moon suits."

"Where is this ship from?"

"Ask the suit yourself. Look at the ship while you ask so the suit can see which way your eyes are pointing."

Helene did that, and the synthetic female voice of the suit said, "This ship is the ARK *Adventure Paradise* from Terra Nova."

"Terra Nova?" Helene said to Tom. "I thought it was Nova Terra."

"In the Ecumene, there's a Terra Nova and a Nova Terra both," Tom said. "There is also a New Earth, an Earth Two, and a New Nova Terra. One thing we didn't take to the colony planets was a lot of creativity."

"I'm just realizing that people on Earth really don't know much about the planets," Helene said. "I sort of think we don't want to know." The rack swung through a curve and headed downward toward the passenger terminal.

"We know about the planets because of the work we do," Tom said. "Otherwise, I suppose Moon Men wouldn't take any interest in anything off the Moon. Of course, if it weren't for travel between the planets nobody would need us, and there wouldn't be any Moon Men."

The rack was automatically shunted to a side rail and came to rest outside of the terminal building. Tom put Helene's suitcase on the ground, then helped her out of the seat. They found Gregor and Yeni waiting to ride back to air town.

"Hi, you two!" Yeni said. "Helene, you look *nice!* I love your hair!"

"Hello, Yeni," Helene said, and everyone exchanged greetings around. "Yeni, we were gone a long time. Are you just finishing up from the reception?"

"You bet. We like to party around here. I'm so sorry you missed it. We're going to the hotel for our honeymoon."

"You should get your suit painted tomorrow, though," Gregor said. "A pretty girl like you should have something better than plain white. I have to get this tuxedo thing off. I usually have some kind of hula-girl painting."

"Not any more, sweetie," Yeni said. "Helene, are you staying the night in the village?" Helene nodded, and Yeni continued, "That's nice. You two get some sleep, now. I doubt if we will." They climbed into the monorail rack and were carried up and away as Tom and Helene waved.

The ship from Terra Nova had landed and a rollagon bus full of passengers was pulling up to the terminal as they started walking back to the village. Helene tried to pull her suitcase behind her but the wheels would not roll in the dust. Eventually Tom picked it up.

Helene walked carefully, trying out various gaits and learning how the ring joints in her suit were articulated. "You know," she said, "this is kind of a lot of work, wearing this thing."

"Oh, you'll get used to it. After a while you won't notice it at all."

"I suppose at some point I'll be able to dance in this suit."

"And do pretty much anything else," Tom agreed. "The only real problems we have with suits are trying to use equipment that was designed to be used by people in air. Look ahead there, that's the Easterday family grounds. If you get lost, ask your suit for directions. Looks like a lot of them are in bed already."

"I'm ready for bed," Helene said. "How do I brush my teeth ... oh, wait, I think I know what the answer is. Is there a doorway marked on the ground that we have to go through or something?"

"Not for members of the family. Hold up a moment." Tom muttered in quickspeak, then said,

"Okay, you're a member of the family now. Just step over the pink lights."

"Tom, what did I just get signed up for?"

"Nothing, nothing at all. I just told the network to put you in the family group so you have access to all the Easterday family resources. Your account will be deleted when you go back to Earth."

The plain of Sinus Amoris was so flat that Helene could see the whole village. With the sunshades folded, she could see a few small buildings here and there, but mostly the village was empty flat ground punctuated with short posts sticking up from the ground, and a few cabinets and shelves. The Moon Men were at various stages of their day depending, she supposed, on what shift they were on. A few squares away, a group of space-suited figures was dancing a silent, frenetic jitterbug, presumably listening to recorded music they weren't sharing with anyone else. Nearby, most of the people were sleeping, sitting on the ground plugged into one of the posts, propped up against their backpacks with their feet stretched out.

Tom led her to a circle of Moon Men, sitting on the ground facing each other. Helene immediately pictured them sitting around a campfire, although there was nothing in the middle of the circle. Many of them looked curiously at her suitcase. One rose gracefully and waved. "Hi, Tom," he said. "We heard about the wedding. Helene, welcome! We're glad you could stay with us tonight."

Helene looked at Tom. "Look at him and say 'Suit, identify,'" Tom said. "We don't usually do introductions among ourselves." She did so and there was a display of boxes in her helmet. The box for "Harper Easterday" was highlighted, with a line pointing to "Thomas Easterday" that was labeled "Father Of". Other boxes showed his mother, two uncles, a sister, a brother-in-law and some nephews and nieces. As she turned to face other people in the circle, the highlighted box changed.

"Hi, Dad, Mom, everybody," Tom said. "Folks, I guess I should introduce Helene, since she just got her suit. She's the salesman for a bunch of Earth co-ops I buy from. She's going out tomorrow to talk with some other customers, so she came here for the evening. Helene, this is my family. The part of it in Sinus Amoris, I mean."

"Hi," Helene said uncertainly.

Harper frowned. "Helene, you got fired from your job? I'm sorry about that! What happened? There are no details given."

Helene glanced sharply at Tom, who looked abashed. "I've been trying not to mention that we know that," he said. "But yeah, when you registered the suit, the network exposes all of the news about you. The firing happened before you got the suit, so the network only knows what the hotel reported."

"So much for being a woman of mystery," Helene said bitterly. "How about if I don't talk about why I was fired? Anyway, I'm thinking if I can come back with some orders, they'll take me back."

"I'm sure they will," Harper said generously. "There's always a market for food here, especially fancy food. Tom just sells to other Moon Men because he's a bit of a snob, but we have a lot of ships' chandlers here who supply the ship companies, and their passengers do nothing but eat for four days on their trips."

"I didn't know you only sold to Moon Men," Helene said.

"Passengers on those ships just pound down food like there's no tomorrow," Tom said. "There's no satisfaction in giving them good food, they have no discrimination. I like people to appreciate what I sell."

"Hello, Helene. I'm Louisa," Tom's mother said. "We were just talking and getting the kids ready for bed. I'm so glad you could join us. I'm sorry about the scare you had with your old suit. It looks like Tom got you a pretty nice one."

"Everybody chipped in for the suit," Tom said. "I just took her into air town." He turned to Helene and said, "Here, let me help you sit down. It's kind of a skill." The others moved out of the way to make a space in the circle and he lowered her gently down with both hands. Tom and his father sat at the same time, with elegant ease.

"Isn't it going to get cold, sitting here?" Helene asked.

"It won't get any colder than it is right now," Louisa said. "Minus 154, I believe. But we're in vacuum and that's an insulator. You'll be fine."

"Moon suits have extra padding in the fanny so you don't lose heat when you're sitting," Tom added. "It's something only we do, different from the kind of space suit you'd get to wear in, you know, space."

"You've thought of everything," Helene said, smiling. A few of the Moon Men had opaqued helmets and were marked on her display as asleep.

54

The others all had little "social" lights inside their helmets to display their faces to each other. Many of them were talking, although Helene could not hear them. She assumed they were chatting with each other.

"We have thought of everything," Tom's father said. "The proof is, we're alive. Helene, welcome again. You're part of the weirdest bunch of people in the Ecumene now."

"I'm just wearing the suit," Helene said. "I'll be going back to Earth. Anyway, you're not weird. I mean, not real weird."

"Oh, don't say that! It's a point of pride with us," Tom said. "Any Moon Man will try to tell you he's a weirdo. Truthfully, I guess we're pretty ordinary. We just like to think we're strange."

"Once you put on the suit," Louisa said, "you're a Moon Man as long as you're here. The environment around a person always shapes them, isn't that so? Well, the Moon environment shapes us *real hard*. When you've been here a week, you'll be one of us. It'll make you nervous not have the suit around you. Wait and see."

A tiny girl in a small Moon suit toddled up. One of the other women sitting in the circle said, "Mika, come back. You need to go to sleep." Helene's display identified her as Tom's niece Mika, daughter of his sister Glory and brother-in-law Roberto, who were sitting together.

"I'm not sleepy, Mommy. Hi, Tom," Mika said. "Helene, you're from Earth, right? Do you like it on Earth? Where are you from? I want to go to Earth."

"I hope you can, honey," Helene said. "I do like it on Earth. I'll give you a tour when you come. I'm from near Chicago."

"I see it!" Mika said, looking up.

Helene looked up at the half-phase Earth. She could not make out any outlines of continents under the clouds. She glanced at Tom, who touched the interface on her arm with his finger. He spoke a couple of incomprehensible words of quickspeak, then said, "Look back to Earth." Her view of the Earth through the helmet glass was replaced with a composite globe image with no clouds. The image rotated and Chicago appeared, marked with a bright dot of light.

Mika's mother Glory stood, grabbed her kid and pulled her back. "You go to sleep!" she said, and when she had put Mika back on the ground, connected the child's suit to cables and hoses coming from one of the posts, and touched a control on the backpack in a position the child could not reach. Mika sat without moving, and although she was presumably expressing opinions, Helene could no longer hear her.

"I think it's time for all of us to sleep," Louisa said. Apparently she was the family matriarch, because there was a chorus of good-nights and the helmet lights began blinking out around the circle.

"Helene, are you ready for bed?" Harper asked.

"Oh, God, yes," Helene said. "It's been a day."

"Then we'll talk again in the morning. Good night." Tom's parents' helmets went opaque, and Helene suddenly realized she was no longer hearing anyone's breathing except Tom's.

"Let's get you plugged in," Tom said. He reached over her and connected her by cables and hoses to a post, moving her suitcase to one side. "Water, power, signal, air if you need it, although I don't think you will."

"What if I roll over in my sleep? What if I want a drink? What if I start screaming because I have this dream I'm trapped in a Moon suit and can't get out?" She paused, then said "Oh, yeah. I know where to get answers. I guess I don't have to ask you anything, do I?"

"I suppose not, but I hope you will anyway."

"Tom?" she said sleepily, "Thanks for letting me stay with you."

"You're sure welcome. But later on, you're going to tell me why you're really here and not in the hotel, right?"

Helene sighed. "Yeah, there's a story. But not now, okay?"

"Sure thing."

"Tom? Leave your link with me on, will you? I need to hear some noise. I still feel really isolated in this thing."

"I'll listen to you, too. I'll set it up so that we can hear each other breathing, but if either one of us snores, it will turn down the volume automatically."

She giggled. "All right. Good night."

"Good night."

Helene sat awake for a few minutes, gazing up into the starry mystery of the sky. Tom was asleep, and eventually she slept as well.

The Earthlight cast their unmoving shadows on the ground.

5: Breakfast in the Night

The Easterday family was large and all of them worked the first shift. A half dozen of them were on kitchen duty for breakfast and had been up for an hour when a family-wide bell woke the rest. It was still Night, of course, and would be for another thirteen days, but one by one they stretched, unplugged themselves from cables and hoses and stood in one smooth motion.

Helene was awakened by the same bell. She tried to stand but forgot to unplug herself, and was yanked to one side. She settled to the ground with the eerie slowness of lunar gravity and cursed. Tom was standing next to her and chuckled. "Good morning, Helene," he said. "You slept well." He helped her back into sitting position.

"Hello, Tom. I was up a couple of times during the night," she said. "Help me up, will you?"

"You weren't awake all that long," Tom said. "Once after about three hours and once at five hours, but only for a couple of minutes. Actually, why don't you stay seated for a few minutes? It looks like you need a bath."

"And how are my bowel movements?" Helene asked between clenched teeth. "Acceptable to you?"

"That all looks good," Tom answered pleasantly. "So here, you sit up, keep your arms at your sides and ask the suit to give you a bath while you're still plugged into the family water. If you get the bath anywhere else it costs more."

Helene did so without comment. Warm water sluiced over her entire body except the hair on her head, delivered to her skin by what was apparently a network with hundreds of little pores. The water rinsed under the folds of her breasts, washed between her toes and sprayed her face. She heard a pump removing the water from whatever collection points it had gone to, and then warm air blew out of the same set of pores to dry her. "Okay," she said, somewhat ungraciously, "that's pretty nice. How come you don't need a bath?"

"I had one yesterday before I met up with you," Tom said. "We usually get a bath every three days – it gets a little expensive to take one more often than that."

"How did you know I needed one? I mean, wait, I know that. How did the suit know I needed a bath?"

Tom hesitated while text flowed up the inside of his helmet. "I never thought about it," he finally said, "but apparently the suit decides you need to wash by looking at readings from a skin galvanometer. That's interesting."

Helene was a little unsteady when she finally got to her feet. She happened to kick her suitcase. The suitcase instantly shattered into fragments and the contents settled to the ground. Her clothes survived but several other articles shattered as well.

"I should have thought of that!" Tom said. "Helene, this is my fault. That suitcase was made of nylon or something, right? That's what happens to nylon when it gets supercooled. I'm guessing your clothing is cotton? I think that will be okay."

Helene picked up a blouse and said, "The cloth is still good but the buttons have cracked off. My shoes are ruined, too. All the underwear with elastic is little crackly pieces now."

"You'll have to go through air town to get home. We'll get you some new clothes then."

"No, no, you've done enough for me. I travel a lot on my job so I never take anything I can't afford to lose. Let's get breakfast." She scraped her possessions together into a smaller pile and regarded it for a moment, but could not think of anything tidier to do.

The Easterdays owned four food carts. The adults stood and gossiped, facing each other, while the kids ran around between them. Breakfast that day was fruit-filled pierogies, with chubby bite-sized sausages and coffee. Tom introduced her to the aunts and uncles who were cooking that day. Aunt Carletta stood at the first cart, her arms inserted into the ports and her hands bare. She and Tom talked about yesterday's wedding as Helene watched her expertly flatten little circles of dough, add a spoonful of blueberry filling and fold and pinch the dough around it without a single wasted motion. She popped the pierogies into a pot of boiling water.

Next to her, Uncle Julio took the boiled pierogies (from a previous batch Carlene had passed to him) and fried them in butter on the cooktop until they were brown, added a dollop of sour cream and arranged four of them in a sixpack with a sausage and a ball of toasted bread, which he pushed out through the pass-through valve. Tom took it and helped Helene snap it into the fitting on her helmet, along with a flask of coffee.

"Tom, Carletta, Julio," Helene said after a few minutes, "this is fabulous. Thank you! Do you eat like this all the time?"

"You're welcome! We do eat good," Carletta said. "Lots of different kinds of food, of course."

"When Carletta is cooking for breakfast, it's always pierogi," Julio said. "I tried making the pierogi one time and got strawberry goop all over everything. I don't have the magic fingers, you know?"

"I'm starting to see why you import all that fancy food from Earth."

"Well, most of it's for ship passengers, of course," Julio said. "We raise chickens, pigs and goats here – there're some big farms over in Maury crater we buy from – but cows never did adapt to living on the Moon. We have carniculture, but you can't get a decent steak that way, so we buy a lot of beef from Earth."

"I know, the expensive stuff," Helene said. "High end. I've seen the orders."

"Sure. It doesn't make sense to pay all that freight and save a few sequins on cheap meat."

"We grow some herbs up here," Tom said, "but it makes better sense to get dried spices from you. Same thing with vegetables – we raise a lot here, but we get specialty items from you."

"Well," Helene said, "I'm off today to try to talk a bunch of importers into buying more food from my co-ops."

"Didn't you get fired from that job?" Carletta asked.

"Oh, my God! Does everybody on the Moon know I got fired?"

"Just the Moon Men," Carletta said peaceably. "In air town, they don't care about each other."

"Well," Tom said judiciously, "I think it's just that in air town, they don't have any easy way to find out about each other."

"I'm hoping if I bring in some orders, they'll take me back," Helene said miserably.

"Go for the ships' chandlers," Carletta said. "Passengers love to hear they're getting real Earth food. It's a prestige thing, even though the food we grow here is just as good. Guys like Tom who sell to Moon Men, they don't care where it comes from."

"I'll buy more from you," Tom said. "There's always a market for fancy spices."

"Tom, don't give me pity, okay? I'm a professional. I can sell."

Julio and Carletta exchanged glances. "Oh, Helene, Tommie's in love with you," Carlene said. "Anybody can see that. Let him buy some spices from you if he wants to."

"How can you just bust out and say things like that? That's rude!" Helene said.

"True, though," Julio said. "You look at his heart rate and skin conductivity and stuff when he's looking at you, it's pretty obvious. Not to mention that we've known Tommie since he was born. He always did have an eye for the ladies."

"Tom, don't buy from me unless it makes sense for your business, you hear? I'm going back to Earth in a couple of weeks."

"I just switched us so we're talking privately," Tom answered. "I won't buy anything I can't make a profit on, I promise. And yes, I know this relationship isn't going anywhere."

"Relationship? There is no relationship! Aren't you going to say something about how they're wrong and you're not really in love with me?"

"Why would I say that?" Tom asked. "You can see my metrics just like anybody can. But look, this is my problem and I understand that. I'll deal with it."

Helene stared at him. "I don't understand you people at all. Look, do you think I'm in love with you?"

"You haven't been wearing a Moon suit long enough to establish a baseline, so I can't tell," Tom said. "I guess you are still kind of a woman of mystery, at that. *Are* you in love with me?"

"No. Tom, you're a nice guy and if you ever decide to emigrate to Earth, look me up. Until then, back off. I'm going out to do business, pure business."

"Not much chance of me going to Earth," Tom said ruefully. "I guess you're safe."

"All right, I'm out of here."

"Finish eating and take the sixpack off before you go," Tom said. "You'll look pretty silly walking around with it sticking out of your helmet."

"How about the coffee? Can I keep that?"

"Yeah. That's why the drink cylinder lies flat against your chest, lots of people like to keep drinks with them."

After a little conversation with her suit and a few more bites, Helene re-established contact with the people around her, detached the sixpack and

63

handed it back to Julio, then started walking toward the monorail terminal.

Behind her, the voices of Julio, Carletta and Tom vanished. They were having a private conversation with each other. Helene deduced they were gossiping about her.

6: Ringing Doorbells, in Vacuum

There was a different Moon Man working at the passenger terminal, who set Helene up with a monorail chair. This time, Helene was able to see what the fare would have been to ride the passenger car, and was grateful to get in for free.

The monorail linked every settlement on the Moon. In the low gravity, even a fairly spindly rail was strong enough to carry passengers and freight, and a sunshade was all that was needed to keep the rail cold enough to be superconducting during the Day. Riding alone for an hour, swinging beneath the rail as it rose and fell over the cratered gray landscape, Helene learned all over again that the Night sky was endlessly fascinating and the ground was, mostly, not.

She soared over the edge of Mare Crisium Field, another busy passenger terminal. Her first call was a Moon Man distribution business called Chun How Wholesalers, although oddly enough the company seemed to be run entirely by Moon Men with Swedish names. They regularly bought steaks and sea food from her company.

Mare Crisium village looked exactly like Sinus Amoris village, down to the ranks of sleeping Moon

Men whose families were not on shift, parties with dancing and a gathering of space-suited figures for some private purpose that her suit would not tell her. She flew over her customer's warehouses near the field, some enclosed but most of them just sunshaded rows of storage racks loaded with containers of food. She came to ground at the terminal building and let her suit call for a taxi.

The taxi was made for Moon Men and did not have any seat, just an arrangement of pipes that she could sit on. It turned out to be perfectly comfortable and as it rolled away at no great speed, Helene rehearsed her sales pitch.

*   *   *

"You're wearing a real suit!" Oscar Amundsen said when they met. "I thought you were from Earth ... oh, wait, I see ... you've been fired? Don't get me wrong, I really appreciate your company sending somebody out to talk to me in person, but how can you take orders if you don't work there?"

"I was hoping I could bring back some orders and they'd re-hire me."

"Ah. That's a little under the table, isn't it? Well, we may be able to work something out. I always need steaks, tuna, caviar and other stuff I can't get on the Moon. I buy from several companies but I can give you the business if you can work with me on the price." He named some sample prices.

"I have to make a profit!" Helene said. "I mean, the company has to make a profit. I can't meet that."

"We can wiggle a little on the price, maybe ten percent."

"That's not half of what you've been paying!"

"And you're in a real poor position to bargain, aren't you?"

*   *   *

Mare Crisium Ship Supply, another Moon Man-run company: "You guys sold us some bum meat last year. Beat it."

*   *   *

The air town for Mare Crisium Field was Swift Crater City. Helene was carried up to the rim and checked through the airlock at the speed Moon Men expected – her suit was her complete identification. She barely wasted a glance at the town and took a taxi to Chandrashekar Caterers, to meet with Rajit Saran, the president. His offices were low on the crater rim, only about one story over the floor. He took her out to a patio and served coffee.

"I must say, you're the only Moon Man I can ever recall who came to me as a salesman," he said.

"I'm not really a Moon Man. I just have this suit. It's kind of a long story, but I'm from Earth."

"Now that I think about it, Moon Men ladies don't have beautiful long hair like yours," Rajit said. "When you come in here in that suit with the helmet off, it really emphasizes your face. In a very good way."

"You've been buying meat and some other things from us," Helene said. "What can I do for you to help your business?"

66

"You can do something to help *me*," Rajit said. "Moon Men ladies are always so interesting, don't you know? It's like a woman in a burka, what is hidden is always fascinating. Why not take off that clumsy suit and let's conduct business in nicer clothing?"

"It takes a technician to get the suit off," Helene said, with a strained smile.

"I know a hotel here that does that," Rajit said.

She rose and left.

*   *   *

Fat Jack's Foods was run by a fat fellow named Maurice, who welcomed Helene into his messy office. "It's nice to see somebody from Earth!" he said. "I'm an Earthman too. Where are you from?"

"Chicago."

"Chicago! I'm from Chicago! I mean, Hammond, close enough, right? Man, I wish I could go back. I've been on the Moon too long and my heart's so soft by now I'd probably die the day I touched down, but I really miss it. Is Corey's Pizza still downtown?"

"It is," Helene said. "I went there with a girlfriend a couple of months ago."

That set Maurice off on a long, rambling string of reminiscences about restaurants, good food, old friends and the long-ago failed romance that sent him off to the Moon to make his fortune.

Finally, Helene was able to break in to ask, "So, how about some good Earth food for the passengers? Food with a *context*, right? Food with soul? What can I provide for you?"

"Oh, business isn't so good now. I can't order any more than what I'm already getting."

*   *   *

Bandarlog Ship Chandlers in air town: "They have a very distinctive cuisine on Prester John, and we get a lot of requests for that kind of food from ships going to or from there. Now, it's too expensive to actually get food from any of the colony planets. For Earth, we have to pay to have the cargo shot up on the mass driver, but from any other planet we would have to pay that and also have to pay to have the food brought here on a ship. Now, I know a guy in the customs office. If we could get food from you and have it re-documented as coming from Prester John ..."

*   *   *

Helene rode the monorail back over mountains to Lacus Somniorum, a cargo field not used for passengers. The field was thickly surrounded by factories and warehouses swarming with robot forklifts supervised by Moon Men. Her customer was Sunny Meadow Farms in Maury crater. She cycled through the air lock with the usual quickness, but then was nonplussed to have to wait, her arms up, while robot arms scrubbed her suit and rinsed her with germicides. Presently she was dried off, the inner airlock door opened and she looked out on the crater.

There was no city, just a little town built near the middle, surrounded by farm fields. The sky in Maury crater was dark, but the crater floor was

68

brilliantly lit with crop lights. A taxi carried her along kilometers of farm lanes, past fields of soybeans, corn, spinach and other crops a city girl could not identify.

All of the agriculture she passed was "aeroponics," with the plants suspended from racks. The plant roots were exposed to the air, and little squirting robots shuttled back and forth on rails, coating the roots with water and nutrients. Under identical conditions, every plant grew to exactly the same height as its neighbor.

The air smelled bad, with a barnyard odor coming from, her suit informed her, feedlots raising hogs, turkeys, goats and chickens.

As she neared her customer's offices, however, the aeroponics racks ended suddenly and she was faced with a farm field of plain dirt, with something – maybe onions, she thought – growing in a normal way with only the greens showing above ground. Various robots worked the field. Her taxi rolled to a stop in front of a black man dressed in farmer's overalls. Costumed, really, Helene thought: the overalls were spotlessly clean.

"Welcome to the only dirt firm on the Moon!" he said. "You must be Helene. I'm Don Henderson. Take a look, you won't see anything like this again!"

"Hi," Helene said. "Wow, where did you get all the dirt?"

"I started by importing two cubic meters of real Mississippi gumbo mud, to be a starter culture," Henderson said. "I made a composter and broke down a few tons of food scrap, bought bones from the hog farm and made bone meal, and added hog and chicken manure. Then I plowed it all into the Moon dust that was here and let the bacteria spread and make it all into soil. Now, I've got a dirt farm!" He added confidentially, "The secret of good dirt is, it's *dirty*. It's full of manure and all kinds of smelly stuff. People expect it to be dirty. Did you know the word 'dirt' comes from the Old Norse *drit*, which meant shit? I've got the really *drit*-y dirt. It's a selling point!"

"It's nice, I think," Helene said, stepping out of the taxi on the side away from Henderson.

"It's a gold mine, or will be in a couple of months," Henderson said. "People pay extra for Earth food. 'Earth' *means* 'dirt,' right? I can't say my stuff was 'grown on Earth' but I can say it's 'grown in earth' and I can sell to the fanciest ships' stewards for a fraction of what you charge. No offense, I hope, but I'm not going to need to import any more vegetables from Earth."

"Well, *drit*!" Helene said.

*   *   *

"Pineapples are basically weeds," Parinya Hongam of Fruit Universe told Helene. She was a small, elegant woman in a slit dress, looking very out of place in a vast orchard of fruit trees and crops. "They grow fine here, or anywhere. I know we used to buy them from you, but we don't need them anymore. We do get requests for some exotic Earth fruits, not really for any reason except that the ship chefs want to put fancy names on the menu. Can you supply canistels or horned melons or feihoas?"

"I don't know what those are," Helene said. "We could probably put in some crops."

"Oh, no. I only need a box here and there."

*   *   *

On the way back to Sinus Amoris the suit offered to play music or movies, but Helene rode in silence, looking up at the stars and the clouds moving over Africa. She trudged back to the village from the passenger terminal and met Tom.

"Ask me how my day went," she said,

"I can see. Boy, that's rough," Tom said.

"I said, *ask* me how my day was," Helene said in a low, dangerous voice.

"Oh. Um, how was your day?"

"If I could pack in it those little toilet cartridges and sell them to a broker, I'd be rich," Helene said. She told him over supper (eighteen bites of *The Bird Hops from Tree to Grassland*). She told him later, when they were relaxing on the ground at home. She continued to tell him until they went to sleep.

Tom listened, looking at her face. His family, their voices restricted to each other, discussed that and nodded knowingly.

7: Moon Men are Blinded with Science

Breakfast for the Easterday family was spoonfuls of oatmeal and berries, bacon cleverly tied into bite-sized knots, melon balls and coffee. Helene and Tom sat together on the ground, chatting with a few of the two dozen family members spread around them. A woman wearing a suit painted with a scene

71

of sunset over a lake walked up and Tom said, "Hey, Susanna. How are you?"

"I'm fine," she said. "I wanted to talk to Helene for a moment. Helene, I'm Susanna. I'm a second cousin to Tom."

"Hi," Helene said. "I met you at the wedding. I mean, I didn't actually meet you, but ..."

"But I got drunk and they talked about me, right?" Susanna said. "Hang on a moment." She walked over to the food carts, manned this morning by other Easterday family members, and accepted two six-packs and a flask of coffee. She plugged one six-pack into the helmet of her suit, and returned to sit by Helene.

"I'm sorry," Helene said. "I didn't mean to bring that up."

"Don't worry about it," Susanna said. "You're new around here, so let me just say that if you're going to be a Moon Man, you've got to learn to let the embarrassments go."

"Well, I'm just here temporarily. But people forget your embarrassments after a while."

"Nah. People forget but the network never does. For the rest of my life, anybody who's interested can find out that I've gotten drunk at three weddings – so far, I mean – and done a bunch of other stuff. Actually, that's what I wanted to talk about. Girl, you had some kind of day yesterday, didn't you? What a bunch of jerks!"

"So now everybody can see that, too?"

"If you know how to ask, which we all do. Anyway, I know a guy here who is a buyer for a ship's chandler, and he's not a customer of yours now but I can set you up with an appointment if you want. He's an ex-boyfriend but we're still friends and I guarantee he's not as much of a jerk as those other guys."

"I wouldn't guarantee that," Tom said. "I used to play poker with that guy."

Tom's sister Glory happened to be in their conversation group. "Is that Jacque Weatherall? I used to know him, haven't seen him for a few years though."

"Yeah," Susanna said. "He's a buyer for Quiboon Supply now. They're pretty big, they have contracts with a couple of ship lines."

Helene took a deep breath. "Yes, I would, and thanks," she said. "But could you make it tomorrow instead of today? I feel like I've really got to take a day off."

"Sure thing. Hey, it's Wednesday, which is my day off. You want to come meet the Wednesday Ladies Club?"

"What's that?"

"Women who have Wednesday off. We get together to do stuff."

"I wondered about that," Helene said. "Another thing you don't seem to have here is the concept of weekends."

"The ships come and go twenty-four hours a day," Tom said. "Everybody's on one time shift and gets one day off a week. I'm a Wednesday myself. I'll tell you another thing the Wednesday Ladies Club does, though. They get humiliated by the Wednesday guys playing Pitch and Toss."

"In your dreams, loser," Susanna said cheerfully. "*We* have teamwork. *You* bump into each other running in circles."

"Pitch and toss?" Helene asked. "You mean like matching pennies?"

"No, it's a game we play that involves tossing into the pitch," Susanna said. "Also dancing, which is another thing little boys aren't good at. Anyway, we have a women-versus-men game today. Want to be on the team?"

"I've never played before. I don't even know what it is," Helene said.

"See, that's the beauty of it. You will *still* be better than any of the Wednesday Mister Machos, like Tom here."

"Helene, if you come to this game you will watch us blind 'em with science," Tom said. "Oh, and there's a rock fall after lunch, too. Actually, this would be a good day for you to take off. Lots of entertainment today."

"A rock fall?"

"We'll tell you about it, it's a thing we do," Susanna said. Another woman came up, a black lady with a cheerful grin, wearing a design of elongated, stylized green dancers against a yellow background, with an abstract design in her wedding-oval. No one introduced her, but Helene's display identified her as Gloria Beacon.

"Gloria," Susanna said, "can we put Helene on the team for today?"

"No problem!" Gloria said. "Helene, if you're done with breakfast why don't you pop off that sixpack and we'll take you to the field? I'm the captain for today."

"I thought I had one more bite," Helene said, twisting the knob.

"No, you're done."

"I will never get used to how everybody knows everything I do," Helene said, detaching the sixpack. She handed it back to Tom's cousin Hector at the food cart.

"I went to Earth once," Gloria said, "and I could never get used to being lonely like that. Come on, we'll take you to the field and show you how to play. I'll pick up my kids on the way."

"Are you going too, Tom?" Helene asked.

"In a little bit," Tom said. "Us Wednesday guys have got to plan our victory party, you know."

"Your pity party, you mean," Susanna said.

"Hey, we win 54.5% of the time!" Tom said.

"Now that's just rude!" Gloria said with asperity.

"I guess you can just look up the win-loss records," Helene said. "Like everything else."

"Of course we can," Gloria said. "But it's bad sportsmanship to say it like that. Now we're mad, boys, so I'm pretty sure today will even up the odds. Don't say I didn't warn you!"

Gloria collected her two little children, and with Susanna formed up a party of Wednesday women and their kids who were too young for school. Some of the women were carrying baby balls as well. They stepped into the "street" and ambled out to the playground, another featureless expanse on the edge of the nearly featureless village. The equipment there was unfolded and laid on the ground. They worked together to erect a set of monkey-bars and other playground equipment for the kids.

"Why don't you just leave this set up?" Helene asked. "I mean, it's not like you're short of room."

"If we set it up permanently, it would, you know, be there," Susanna said. "If everybody did that, pretty soon there would be stuff everywhere you look. I mean, it wouldn't make much difference for this, because every shift uses the playground, so it's set up most of the time. But it's not hard to take it down at the end of one shift and set it up next shift."

They parked the kids in the playground, with one mother keeping watch on them all. "The kids are playing exactly the same game here they play back home," Helene said with satisfaction, watching them. "It's called Let's Run Around Like Small Crazy People."

"You know it. Here, on Earth and on absolutely every other planet," Gloria said. "You'd think they would be tired after a few hours but they rest for twenty minutes and they're ready to go again. Me, not so much."

They went to the athletic field and set up the "pitch," which was a circular chain-link fence twenty-four meters in diameter and ten meters high. There was one opening on either side, just big enough for one Moon-suited person, which Helene's display identified as a "wicket."

"Okay, let's show you how it's done," Gloria said.

"Isn't there a ball of some kind?" Helene asked.

76

"Oh, no. On the Moon, if you throw a ball it can go clean over the horizon, and if it's on the ground it doesn't roll too well in the dust. Can't make a game out of that. No, we're going to toss ..." – she looked around – "Sandara, here." One of the other women grinned and walked closer.

"Hi, I'm Helene," Helene said. "I'm new here so she has to explain everything."

"I know," Sandara said. "Hi."

In Helene's helmet, an overlay image suddenly made Sandara appear to be outlined with a bright red border. "I'm Captain for this game, so I get to pick who will be the 'Bright,'" Gloria said. She raised her voice slightly and said, "Ladies, let's toss her once to show Helene what we do."

Four women grabbed Sandara by the arms and legs. Gloria said, "Ready. Steady. Go." They launched her up into the star-spangled sky and a timer display appeared in Helene's helmet, counting the seconds.

Sandara soared up, spinning a little, her arms wide and her legs together like a high-board diver. She reached her apogee and slowly fell back. The others raced to get under her and caught her precisely with eight hands. They lowered her gently to the ground and her red outline blinked off. Helene's timer stopped at 28 seconds.

"Okay, so during an inning, everybody has to be outside of the pitch," Gloria said. "The way to make a score is, I turn somebody on to be the Bright and then we toss her over the fence into the pitch. Once she leaves the ground, we've got twenty or thirty seconds to get four players into the pitch to catch her. The other team is trying to get four players in there, too.

Nobody's allowed to block the wickets. If our team catches her, we get one point. If the other team catches her, they get two points, so we don't want that. If nobody catches her, she's not in danger because it's easy enough to land on your feet, but we lose four points and the other team loses three. So both sides have to work together to make sure somebody catches the Bright. Once the play is over, everybody has to get out of the pitch and the other team picks a new Bright. Okay so far?"

"I guess," Helene said dubiously.

"Then one more thing." Cheerful Latin music filled Helene's ears, strongly rhythmic. "It's like for basketball, you're not allowed to move without dribbling the ball? In this game, you have to be dancing all the time. If you don't stay with the beat, the referee will throw you out. You can be as fancy as you feel like, but just stepping from one foot to the other is good enough. Try it."

Helene stepped back and forth, and the display in her helmet gave her feedback on how well she was doing, measured in the number of milliseconds between a beat in the music and the time each foot touched the ground. Gloria watched the same display in her helmet and finally said, "Good enough. One other thing – don't touch or bang into anybody else, that's not allowed. There are a bunch of other rules, of course, but you just go where everybody else goes and try to get inside the pitch if you're close to the wicket when the Bright goes up, and you'll be fine."

Helene stopped dancing. "I don't have to play. I can just watch. I don't want you to lose."

"You're here and you're a Wednesday, so we want you to play," Gloria said. "Come on, it's fun. If you can't do anything else, I'll make you the Bright. The Bright does nothing except maybe trash-talk the guys while she's in motion."

Several other women had arrived at the field, and then the men trotted up in a double line. Helene looked at them and said in a low voice, "Suit, have those guys been drinking beer already?"

"Yes," the suit said, and in her helmet view each man was labeled with his blood-alcohol level. Tom was sober but several of the others had worked up a pretty good load considering that it was early morning for the first shift.

There was one female referee and one male; to Helene's eyes their suits were surrounded by a yellow outline. They took up positions away from the pitch, and the two teams spaced themselves to form an even circle around the perimeter of the pitch, men on one side and women on the other, all facing outward. Apparently it didn't matter how many players were on each team as long as both teams were the same: four men were left out and stood to one side providing infield chatter.

The referees chose and started the music, a popular tune in a style Helene was not familiar with, possibly from one of the colony planets. She stepped from one foot to the other in place. Some of the women did more ambitious steps, still standing in place.

The referees picked the women's team to start by consulting a random number generator, a whistle was blown and Sandara's suit lit up again. Gloria

79

took off running to the left, her feet still moving to the dance rhythm, and in a moment everyone was in motion.

Gloria had not mentioned that the team danced forward and backward, trying to confuse the men, and continuously tossed the Bright between them. Sandara, true to her mission, kept up a steady stream of chatter aimed at goading the men. Helene danced after the pack, trying to keep her rhythm.

At a signal from Gloria, Sandara was lofted high into the sky by the women who happened to be holding her, toward the inside of the pitch. Helene froze for a moment, looking around, and discovered she was second-closest to the wicket. She ran pell-mell for the opening until a whistle sounded in her helmet. "Off-rhythm!" the woman referee called. "One minute penalty." Helene was forced to run away from the pitch, then watched as four women and six men danced inside, careful not to jostle each other. Sandara was caught by three women and one man. Since the women had the majority, they got the point.

Everyone danced out of the pitch, took up the circular formation, and at a whistle, one of the men became the Bright and was tossed.

Helene was allowed to re-enter the game for the next inning. The referees switched the music to a waltz, which disrupted everyone's concentration, and the Bright was almost but not quite dropped.

A game was sixteen innings. Helene was the Bright for the eleventh inning. She kept her arms and legs tightly together, her eyes wide, and was tossed like a spinning bundle of lumber. She had been too distracted to listen to the Brights previously, and in the confusion of being tossed between the fast-moving women, discovered she could not think of anything to yell. Finally, as two of the women launched her up toward the pitch, she just hollered "Yeah! You guys stink!"

"That doesn't work for Moon Men!" Tom yelled as he raced through the wicket. "We never smell each other!"

"You guys are dumb!"

"Okay, might have something there."

"Ahh!" Helene yelled, and was caught by Tom and three other men inside the pitch and lowered gently to the ground. Two points to the men.

The game ended with the women winning, 21-19. Both teams were sweaty and worn, and they joked with each other as they took down the pitch. The rolled-up fence was left on the ground for the next teams to erect.

The men went back into the village for more beer, and the women went to the children's playground to watch the kids, gossip and also to drink beer, which a number of them had thoughtfully stockpiled before hand.

Some of the same women who had been willing to leave their kids on the monkey bars for an hour while they were playing, now had trouble sitting together because they wanted to jump up and catch their offspring whenever the kids tried to show off a trick for Mom. Eventually Helene found herself in a group of women who were less twitchy, seated on the ground off to one side of the park. It included Gloria, who was an experienced mother, and Susanna, who had no kids. Helene had never liked beer that well on Earth and saw no reason to start with flat beer, so she was drinking coffee.

The village grid extended to the playground, and there were several of the utility posts sticking up from the ground. Helene checked the price, found that it was more expensive than the Easterday family outlets, and decided to put off taking a bath. Gloria Beacon, however, plugged herself in and luxuriated in a rinse. "Whew, did I need a day off!" she said. "You gotta work up a sweat before you can relax when you're all tense from working all week, right?"

"You know it!" said a middle-aged woman named Myra, seated next to a woman named Golda. Helene's display identified them as married to each other, and on a second look, she noticed they had matching images of a forest in silhouette over their hearts.

"What do you do, Gloria?" Helene asked.

"I'm a stevedore. I load up cargo on the outbound ships. I mean, I don't load them up, the robots do that. I supervise the robots."

"Gloria and I work together," Myra said. "She does the cargo, I do food and water and supplies, and the ship's stewards get the passengers settled. We all have to coordinate to get everything balanced to within a couple of kilograms. If one side of the ship is heavy, the harbor pilot yells at us. That would be Golda, here."

"Especially," Susanna put in, "because the stewards are supposed to get all of the passengers in their seats for takeoff and there's always one prima donna who decides it's her right to get up and go potty."

"Couldn't you let a computer decide where everything gets stowed?" Helene asked.

"We can and we do," Gloria said, "but there's always last-minute changes and things nobody remembered to list and, you know, stuff that needs an intelligent decision. Last week I was loading the *Tropical Princess* and they had a shipment of live geese to ... whatever planet it was going to, I forget. Anyway, the birds were in wire cages but they were able to move back and forth and I couldn't figure out any way to immobilize them. I finally told the stewards we were going to have to put them right smack on the center axis so they couldn't affect the balance as much, and the only place that had enough space was the passenger dining hall. I made 'em stack up those crates in the middle of the floor and lash them in place, and of course the poor geese were honking and banging into the walls of the crates like crazy, and there was goose poop all over because that's what geese do when they're upset. Once they got up into transfer orbit, the stewards had to move all the crates to a regular cargo hold and get the place cleaned up and deodorized before the lunch meal. They were honking and complaining worse than the geese!" Everybody laughed.

"Helene," a woman named Deloria said, "you need to get your suit painted. When you're wearing plain white, you look like a minister or something. You're from Earth, how about a globe?"

"You can look up in the sky anytime and see Earth," another woman chimed in. "Besides, she's too young and pretty for something as stodgy as that. Maybe a mythological creature? What country are you from, Helene?"

"United States," she said.

"My family came here from Prester John," she said. "I don't know much about Earth countries. What kind of mythological creatures could you use?"

Helene smiled. "Road Runner and Coyote?" she said. "Batman? Anyway, I don't think that's what I want. I'm going back to Earth in a couple of weeks anyway, so it doesn't matter."

"You don't want to be half-dressed for two weeks. Listen, we have some real artists in Sinus Amoris and you've got enough money to get something really good. Why don't you let us connect you up? I mean, even if you go back to Earth you're going to want pictures of yourself to show your friends, right? You should be dressed right."

"Even if?" Helene said. "Of course I'm going back to Earth!"

"Well, how about Tom?" a woman Helene had never met asked. "You're just going to leave him?"

"Tom and I do not have a relationship! We're not dating, we're not not-dating, I just barely know him! What is *wrong* with you people?"

"What did Tom say?" Gloria asked calmly.

Helene was silent for a long moment, then said, "He said he was in love with me and he'd deal with it."

"See," Gloria said, "men aren't real good at relationships. They don't look at all the data. Women, we're better at reading all 38 numbers."

"Oh, my God," Helene said. "38 numbers? You're going to tell me what that means and it's going to be something weird and I'm going to hate it, right?"

"Probably," Deloria said. "38 is how many data points your suit collects about your body, all medical stuff to make sure you're healthy. But when you grow up with it, you can look at somebody else's numbers and see patterns."

"Specifically," Susanna said, "we can see how your numbers change when you're around Tom, and we know you're hot for him."

"Why don't *I* know that?"

"Because you're from Earth and you don't always understand your own feelings. Other people can see things you're not admitting to yourself, honey," Gloria said. "But you'll figure it out eventually."

Helene looked from one woman to another. All had turned on the social lights that let them see each other's faces. She turned her helmet light off. "I've been here three days and already you old biddies from the village are trying to marry me off to a local boy!" Helene said. "I feel like we ought to be down by the river washing clothes together on the rocks or something. This is ... this is the *smallest* small town any city girl ever got stuck in! My great-great-grandparents back in Poland lived in a crammed-up little ghetto and I'm pretty sure they weren't as gossipy as you are."

"You've been lonely and isolated all your life," Gloria said, "and now you have to get used to being in a group of friends who understand you. I know that's hard."

"You'd be surprised how much you don't know," Helene said. She tried to stand up but tilted over, and was caught and pushed upright by the other women. With as much dignity as she could muster, she turned and walked back into the village.

8: A Date, with Falling Rocks

On her way back to the Easterday family grounds, Helene was stopped by a train. She stepped back and watched in bemusement as a line of two dozen unmanned cars trundled out of the lunar East and rolled sedately past her. One by one, the cars pivoted at a slight angle to align themselves with the street grid. They headed for the central square downtown and parked themselves in neat ranks next to the church.

When Helene arrived at the central square, Tom and several other people were already there. "Hey, Helene," he said. "Let's grab a car. The rock fall won't be for another hour yet, but I want to make sure we've got a car to get there."

"Oh, that sounds too exciting for me," Helene said. "A rock fall. Just imagine. What does the rock fall off of?"

"The rock falls out of the sky, makes a hell of a big boom and a new crater."

Her eyes went wide. "My God! Don't you have some way to shoot those down or blow them up or something? What if it hits somebody? Will it hit us?"

"It's okay," Tom said, grinning. "The rock is an asteroid called a 'carbonaceous chondrite' and it's going to fall about thirty kilometers south of here. It's going to fall there because that's where we aimed it. We want this rock to fall – in fact, I'm an investor in this particular rock. Asteroids like that are full of carbon and hydrogen and nitrogen and other stuff that is valuable here, so we knock them out of near-Earth orbits and put them down where we can recover them. It's a terrific show and I'd like to take you to see it."

"Listen, Moonie, if you want a date with me, why don't you just ask me to go to a play or a movie or something?"

"They have theaters in air town. When we go to the movies together we just sit next to each other and watch the same show in our helmets. A rock fall's more fun. Anyway, it's not much of a date. After that I have to go into the shop and work today. But why not go? It's not like yesterday was all that fulfilling for you."

"I thought Wednesday was your day off?"

"I'm the boss. The boss doesn't really get a whole day off, just enough time to lose at pitch and toss and watch this show."

"All right, you silver-tongued devil, you've beguiled me. Do we have to get tickets to watch a rock fall out of the sky?"

"Nope. And Helene ... thanks. I really do appreciate that you're going to do something with me."

"I'm still going back to Earth."

"So you are."

"Where did all these cars come from?"

"We rent them from other towns. When somebody else has a rock fall, we rent some of our cars to them."

"I'm guessing that costs some money?"

"My treat," Tom said.

Tom and Helene climbed on to one car and fitted their suits to the pipe racks. The car rolled along the edge-lighted street to the edge of the village, then sped up and took them bouncing over the rolling landscape south of Sinus Amoris. The other rented cars followed them, along with the cars that already belonged to the village.

The car went faster than Helene would have driven and she was obliged to hold on desperately to the hand rail. Moon Men seemed to have an unlimited appetite for gossip – the whole group spent the trip discussing others who had to work and were not part of the caravan. The village quickly receded beyond the Moon's horizon, and they rolled through the gray dusty landscape, automatically dodging around outcrops and craters.

They arrived at a precisely determined point on a low hill, overlooking a shallow valley which appeared, to Helene's eyes, to be exactly as worthless as any other stretch of Moon dust. They dismounted from the car and stood with other spectators, all of them chattering away to each other.

There were a few Moon Men already at the site, herding a set of robot work vehicles that presumably would start harvesting the asteroid after it crashed in.

"I'd figure you had all the rock you want," Helene said privately to Tom. "Why another one?"

"We can cook the dust with mirrors during the Day and get all the oxygen and aluminum we want," Tom said. "Asteroids like this one have stuff we can't get out of the dust, principally carbon and hydrocarbon compounds and nitrogen. You have to have nitrogen for plants and your body really is happier if you breathe about the same nitrogen/oxygen mix as Earth air. Carbon we need for food and all kinds of businesses. I invested in the ship that searches out Apollo asteroids for the right kind and slings them down here. I should make a little money on it. Two minutes."

"I don't see anything," Helene said, looking into the Night sky.

"This rock's as black as coal, which it almost sort-of is," Tom said. "You wouldn't see it. Ninety seconds. Ask your suit to highlight where it's going to hit – the schedules for these things are public."

Her suit drew a red circle inside her helmet that appeared to rest on a patch of Moon ground a kilometer away. Helene said, "How big is this thing? Is this safe?"

"Only about fifty meters across. We'll be okay. Here we go, now."

She never saw anything come out of the sky. The ground erupted as though the explosion had come from underneath. Dust blasted high into the sky and a visible wave rolled through the solid landscape. The sound, coming half a second after the impact, was reduced by having to come through the insulated soles of her boots but was still shattering.

Boulders leaped and bounced all around the impact. The ground shook so hard that several of the watching Moon Men fell over and bounced themselves. Helene stumbled back and Tom caught her. Everything that went up rocketed so fast it was nearly invisible. Everything that fell looked, in the weak Lunar gravity, like a slow-motion film.

A patter of small rocks hitting the ground sounded like rain. Apparently they had calculated their position well, because nothing larger than sand landed on the Moon Men.

Rocks fell for a solid three minutes. The dust that obscured the stars fell at exactly the same speed, with no air to keep it suspended, and when the explosion was over, it was over all at once. The ground was exactly as still as it had been before. The work vehicles moved in and began sifting for pieces of the black rock.

"Okay, Tom," Helene said, "you know how to show a girl a good time. I have to admit that was impressive."

"Thanks," he said.

"A cheap date, too. Come to think of it, what do you Moon Men spend money on? You don't seem to have much of anything, really, except what's in your suits."

"We have each other."

"That sounds like a slogan."

"Ouch, guilty. Yeah, it is a slogan. True, though. Everybody has to work here, because you have to pay for air and water and food and health insurance and all. I've never heard of an unemployed Moon Man aside from the kids, but if there was one, we'd have to send him to air town. But there really isn't much we can spend money on."

"And I'm the traveling salesman who is trying to make you want to make more money," Helene said. "All of a sudden I see the business strategy problem here."

"Hey, if you're a traveling salesman you're supposed to have a guy in every town, right? Can I be your guy in Sinus Amoris?"

"As long as you stay inside your Moon suit, Tom, you're welcome to call yourself by any title you want. You want to be my beau, my boo, my schnookums, my inamorato if that's a word? Knock yourself out."

"What happens if we're in air and I get out of the suit?"

"Then you behave yourself, lover boy."

Tom was silent for a long moment. "I have to go in to the shop," he said. "Will you come with me? It involves breathing air together, but I'll behave while we're there."

"Of course, Tom," Helene said. "Listen, I'm sorry. I think I sound more snippy than I really am. I'd like to see your shop. I don't actually know as much about spices as I try to sound like I do."

"You don't know your danger. When we get to the shop," Tom said, "every ten minutes or so, smack me across the face if I keep talking about spices, okay?"

"Count on it."

The car took them to a small, windowless building on the edge of the landing field, surrounded by warehouses. The airlock was only big enough for one person at a time. Helene waited outside, looking at the ships on the field being serviced by busy Moon

Men, while Tom cycled himself through. She entered when the door opened again.

There was a teenage girl there with Tom, her helmet off to reveal her pale face and straight blonde hair. Her suit was painted with the logo and name of the local high school team, the Sinus Amoris Sabertooth Tigers. Tom had removed his helmet as well. "Helene," Tom said, "this is Shavon, who works for me when she's not in school."

Helene struggled for a minute to remove her helmet, then shook Shavon's bare hand with her gloved one. "Hi," she said. "Glad to meet you. I'm kind of surprised kids here go to school. I mean, go someplace specific for school. Couldn't you learn everything from displays in your helmet?"

"Hi," Shavon said. "School is just a place in the village but they make us go there."

"Gotta socialize the little monsters," Tom said cheerfully. "Otherwise they grow up feral. Shavon, what have you been working on?"

Shavon waved to a monitor mounted on the wall that showed a list of orders. "Curry masalas," she said. "We've got sixteen orders, I just got them all packed."

"Which masala?"

"Special Garam."

"Okay, good," Tom said. The room was lined with shelves holding sealed plastic bags of spices. At a work table in the center, Shavon had been measuring strongly aromatic powders into a bin, then ladling the mixture into thick-walled, pressure-locked plastic boxes. The full boxes were stacked on one end, and there were a hundred or more empty boxes of the same kind on one of the shelves.

"Listen, Tom, Helene, I've got to go," Shavon said. "Is your car still out there?"

"I think so," Tom said.

Shavon pulled on her gloves and put her helmet on without sealing it. She glanced at the display and said, "Yeah, it is. I have to get to school. Helene, nice to meet you." She sealed the helmet.

"Nice to meet you, too," Helene said, and watched as Shavon cycled herself through the airlock.

When they were alone, Helene asked, "Did she really have to go to school right then?"

Tom retrieved his helmet from a hook on the wall and glanced into it. "No, that was an excuse, I guess," he said.

"For what?"

"I think she thought I wanted to be alone with you. I suppose she's right." He replaced his helmet on the hook.

"How would she know that?"

"This is going to sound like a pickup line," Tom said ruefully, "but my pulse rate went up when I watched you take off your helmet. She must have seen the numbers too."

"You people really are strange, you know that? You can barely stand to touch each other, and at the same time you're in each others' private business every minute of the day."

Tom looked down. "Yeah, we are. I know it."

Helene hung her own helmet on the wall and pulled off her gloves, looking around at the tiny room.

"You mix your spices by hand?" she asked? "I just assumed you'd have packaging machinery."

"There are only 72,418 Moon Men," Tom said. "I don't need any automation to make spices for them."

"Tom," Helene said, smiling, "we need to work on that pronounced ethnic accent you have. Now try to put that in regular language. You should say, 'There are about seventy thousand Moon Men.' Try it!"

"There are about seventy thousand Moon Men," Tom said obediently.

"Very good! We'll have you talking normal in no time."

"Why are 'we' worried about that?"

Helene looked confused. "Oh, just ... I don't know, in case you need to talk everybody-language." She picked up one of the containers of curry powder Shavon had just filled. "This box looks like it's been kicked around a few times."

"It's probably fifty years old," Tom said. "We almost never throw away containers. We hardly ever throw away anything."

"Wouldn't it be easier just to use disposable containers? What, do the customers have to send these back to you when they're empty?"

"They do. On Earth, I think you can pretend that when you throw something away, the bacteria in the landfill will degrade it, or the little forest creatures will eat it or it will sink in the mud or something, right? We can't pretend that. When you throw something out here, it will stay there until the Sun goes nova. So we don't use disposable stuff if we can possibly avoid it." Tom brought out a clean cotton rag and wiped the mixing bin, then cleaned the table top. He moved the filled containers of curry to another shelf and set out various bags of spices from Earth.

"What are you making?"

"Herbes de Provence. Winter savory, summer savory, thyme, rosemary, tarragon. I put in a little bit of a few other ingredients, too, strong-tasting stuff the actual French in Provence would never use. Our tastes are actually slightly different from people on planets. I think it's because we don't have the opportunity to smell food as much, so the taste in your mouth is more important. Anyway, my own mix sells better than what I can get pre-mixed from Earth." He washed his hands at a sink, the water looking syrupy and blobby in the low gravity. He began slitting open bags and pouring spices into the bin. The room filled with warm, delicious odors.

"I take it you recycle those plastic bags?" Helene asked.

"Sure. During the Day, you can melt almost anything with sunlight and a mirror, pretty much free. It's a lot easier to re-use stuff when you don't have to worry about oxidation."

Helene looked around and found a low stool, sized to fit someone wearing a suit. She pulled it over and sat, watching Tom. After a while she asked, "Are all Moon Men as gung-ho about living here as you are?"

"I think so," he said. "There are always some kids who grow up here but want to get away — usually because they're full of teenage hormones, if you want the truth — so their families buy them a ticket out to one of the planets. Or they go away for college and don't come back to stay."

"To Earth?"

"You know, I don't think I've ever heard of a kid going to Earth, although I suppose they could. But they always say all the jobs are out on the colony planets, so that's where they go. Anyway, the ones who stay on the Moon and become adults, they like it here."

"You like it here."

"Yeah, and you don't. I get that." Tom stirred his mixture with a startlingly incongruous wooden spoon.

"Everybody's been nosy but otherwise real nice to me here," Helene said. "I like your family a lot. But the Moon is ... is nothing. Gray dust, no air."

"You won't get any argument about that from me, or any Moon Man. If any Moon Man ever took a walk to commune with Nature, he was drunk. We know it's gray rock."

"Did you ever bring a girl here, to breathe air with you and smell the spices?"

Tom looked up at her. "Actually, no. Maybe I should have, now that you mention it. I've gone to Theophrastus with ladies a few times. They have gardens in the city parks, with flowers you can smell."

"How did those dates work out for you?"

"Pretty well, thank you very much. I'm not exactly desperate, if that's what you're getting at."

She looked at him and smiled. "Then why are you chasing a woman who is unavailable? Tom, I'm from another planet, for pity's sake."

"It's what men do."

"Yeah, women too. Listen, Tom, I've got another ten days or so. Want to have a really short-term affair?"

"No."

"Not up for something spontaneous?"

"Moon Men don't do spontaneous," Tom said.

"I could seduce you." Helene held up her hands and wiggled her fingers. "Look, bare naked female hands! Not even a ring! Back home I'm the girl next door, but up here I'm the sex bomb."

Tom put down his spoon, and carefully fitted a lid over the bin. "Helene, please don't play with me. I'm an easy target and I don't know how this game works. Yes, I'm attracted to you but I'll deal with it."

Helene lowered her hands and looked down. "Oh, God, I'm being a bitch again. Tom, I'm sorry. I'm so sorry. I think wearing this Moon suit affects me. I feel like nothing can touch me in here, like everything human bounces off my shell."

Tom walked toward her. "What are going to do?" Helene asked nervously.

"Bounce off you, probably," he said. But when he held out his arms, she rose into them. They came together with a metallic clang and leaned far forward to allow their faces to meet. They kissed passionately and held each other as though their bodies could touch.

Presently Helene pulled back and smiled. She was about to speak when Tom put a finger to her lips. "No jokes," he said quietly.

"I was going to make a joke," Helene said. "But you're right. Tom my dear, you know me well enough to know what I was going to say. That's ... I mean, no man on Earth ever knew me that well."

"Helene," he said.

"Also you're articulate."

"I said no jokes."

Helene smiled again, and this time her smile was vulnerable and endearing. "Also," she said, "you're articulate." She kissed him again.

Tom pulled her close so that their cheeks could touch, and they held each other without moving. After a long while, he pulled back to look at her face, and his eyebrows went up.

Helene smiled, her eyes half-lidded. It was a conversation.

"Helene," he said, "what actually just happened here?"

"Not much, really," Helene said sadly. "You're still a Moon Man, and I still have to go back to Earth. This is just a summer romance. The difference is, now I don't say 'whee,' I say 'damn'."

"Kiss me again."

"I'll kiss you as many times as you'll let me for ten days," she said, and did. She sat back down. "But I still have to go back. I'm not a Moon Man, I'm just dressed up like one. Tom, Tom, I know you're sweet on me because I'm the exotic woman from another planet, and I have long hair, and because you've seen me in clothes. But there's no future in this."

"That's not how men work," Tom said, pulling up another stool and sitting on it. "Men don't actually fall in love with women for reasons. We fall in love first, and then whatever that woman has, that's what we think the reasons are. I really want to touch your hair, and if somebody asked me I'd say I have a thing for long-haired women, but the truth is, it's just because that's what you've got."

She reached out and took his hand, and put it on her hair. When she took her hand away, Tom still stroked her hair and twined his fingers in it.

Eventually Tom pulled back. "I told you we don't do spontaneous. I still have to get these orders packed."

"Tom, I knew you were going to say that. I can tell what you're thinking, too. I know perfectly damn well you're going to pack up a bunch of containers, put on your gloves and helmet and do a system check, cycle through the airlock, call a car to go to the terminal and ship that stuff off to other Moon Men villages. And you know what? I'm okay with that. I'm better than okay, I'm enchanted with it. Tom, you just got yourself a girl by the sheer power of stodginess."

"You just got yourself a guy by the sheer power of ..." Tom said, and could not finish his sentence.

"By the sheer power of. That's a good way to say it. Kiss me again, then back to work," Helene said. "I'll just look at your bare hands."

"I'm sorry I can't be more spontaneous," Tom said. "I actually have to get these orders out."

"I used to be spontaneous," Helene said, "but I have decided on the spur of the moment to give it up."

9: Lumpy Soft Shapes

It took about an hour for Tom to finish mixing, packing and labeling another forty boxes of spices. His work was interrupted several times for more smooching. Finally he and Helene called for a car, loaded up the boxes and rode out to the terminal building to have them delivered by automated containers on the monorail.

Tom passed the boxes to another Moon Man outside the building, in an area of racks, tables and forklift containers. Various cargoes from all the planets were held and sorted for transshipment to other planets or for distribution to other locations on the Moon. But there was a problem with the paperwork and he was obliged to go into the pressurized building to speak with a clerk. They cycled through the airlock together. Tom did not remove his helmet so Helene didn't either.

Their path took them through the passenger terminal. Everyone, even the business travelers, considered spaceship travel to be a luxury cruise, and was dressed in vacation gear. Hawaiian shirts were popular even with those who would not have known what planet Hawaii was on.

"Tom," Helene said privately, "I've been in a Moon suit for three days and I think I'm starting to go native. People without spacesuits are starting to look weird to me."

"Well, sure. But let's give 'em the benefit of the doubt. Back home," Tom said, "most of these people would be wearing something heavier and stiffer, and they would look a lot better that way."

"I know, right? They wear these loose clown costumes and when they wave their arms, stuff wiggles. But I mean, I'm already used to people who have a smooth, hard shape instead of a lumpy soft shape."

Tom grinned. "Apparently a lot of guys agree with you. You're sure attracting some looks from men with your smooth, hard shape."

Helene swiveled her head and caught men looking at her from all directions. "Good lord, is it like this for all Moon Men women?"

"Pretty much. It's like wearing a chador or a nun's habit. If they can see your face, hiding your body is catnip to a lot of guys. A bunch of these guys are mentally undressing you with a mental can opener."

"Are we going to have to take our helmets off in this building?"

"No, there's an external speaker and microphone on the suit, so you can talk to anybody without exposing yourself. Don't turn on the speaker by mistake – I've embarrassed myself that way a couple of times."

Helene marched steadily ahead, facing stiffly forward. "I think I want to keep a shell around me. Tom, I travel all the time and I'm always walking through passenger terminals. It was never like this on Earth. It was never like this in Theophrastus the last two weeks, when I was walking around in regular clothes."

"Well, sure, in those places you were just a regular pretty girl. Before, all the men would be having little fantasies about rescuing you from a burning building or something, and you would throw yourself at them. Here, they're having fantasies about coaxing you out of your suit, and you would say, 'Oh – Your Name Here – I am madly in lust with your fat, flabby body because I have so little experience I have nothing to compare it to!'"

"For all I know, Tommy me boy," Helene said, turning to look at him while still walking, "*you* are fat and flabby. You've seen me in clothes, but I haven't seen you. However, let me just say that I dated a guy in college who actually was kind of fat and not athletic. It didn't work out, but he was a nice-enough guy and I liked him."

"I totally understand. None of us would chase a woman just for sex because all of us Moon Men guys are deeply into relationships."

"All of you Moon Men guys," Helene said, "are full of baloney."

"Well, yes," Tom said. "In that respect, we're exactly like men everywhere."

They eventually reached the company office where Tom was able to straighten out his shipping account by speaking with a clerk through the external speaker of his suit. Helene stood with her back to the wall and waited, with a sharp eye toward the men sitting on benches who were eyeing her.

Rather than go back through the passenger terminal, Tom led the way down a corridor to a cargo area run by a Moon Man friend of his, who let them cycle out through one of the much larger cargo airlocks. They began walking back toward the village, holding hands.

"Now I'm worried about myself," Helene said. "I step out of the airlock into vacuum and the Night sky and flat dust, and I feel better. Tom, am I going to be permanently weird when I go back to Earth?"

"If you are, it's because you were weird when you stepped off the plane here," Tom said. "Which I think you kind of were, in a good way."

"Come to think of it, it's a little weird to get to the Moon on a shuttleplane with wings, isn't it? Only Earth people get here that way, right? So all of us Earthies start out weird."

"It's not just Earth. Every planet uses that system — a big mass driver and lasers to throw the plane into orbit or up to the Moon, then when you come back you fly down in the same plane. But of course people from other planets leave their shuttleplanes behind when they get into their ships to come here." Tom looked at her with love and said, "But Helene, why *did* you come here? I know we think we're pretty important, but I'm guessing all the ship-supply companies on the Moon don't add up to much compared to the amount of food your company would sell to distributors on Earth. Was it really worthwhile for them to send a salesman here?"

Helene smiled. "Tom, I'm not the best salesman they have — had, I mean — but I'm the best one who was willing to come here, and sales have been pretty flat for a couple of years so they were willing to let me try to pump orders up on the Moon. It's not actually that expensive to come here. I think it cost more to send me by regular jet to Cotopaxi Lift Port in Ecuador, than the lift fare to get from there to the Moon. I mean, Cotopaxi is cheap enough that we can ship chili powder and oregano to you, all the way up here, and still make a profit on the deal. So it wasn't that big of a commitment for the company to send me here."

They were nearing the lines of light that marked the streets of the village. "But Tom," she continued, "I *am* a strange woman, because I wanted to go. The truth about Earth is that we pretty much got our feelings hurt over the last hundred years, when new planets were being discovered all the time, and everybody was leaving Earth to go to them. Everybody on Earth now is the child or grandchild of somebody who didn't want to emigrate. We're the stick-in-the-muds who wanted to stick in our own mud, and we don't like to talk about the Ecumene or hear about it or even think about it if we can avoid it. When I told my parents I was coming here, they started sending me links to stories about spaceships that launched and vanished, shuttles that crashed or blew up, travelers who were abducted or raped or something. It's like, we're a whole planet of cowards trying to close our eyes and pretend space travel didn't happen. Did you know our exports to the Ecumene have been going down every year for a couple of decades? Everything we make on Earth, they're starting to make on the planets, and we're okay with that because it means we don't have to interact with those people."

"But you were brave and came here, and interacted with me," Tom said. "I'm grateful."

"I'm glad I came."

"Helene, are you going to tell me why you were fired?"

"No, Tom, I'm not. Will you let me keep that?"

"Yes. I will trust you with anything you want trust on. But look, let's go back to air town tonight. I don't want to wait."

"You don't need to apologize for wanting me, dear Tom. It's what I want, too. But I'm supposed to go see that guy Susanna wanted to set me up with, tomorrow."

"Have you made an appointment?" Helene shook her head. "Then it will wait. Come on, let's go back to the terminal."

"Don't you need to tell your family you won't be home, or something? Oh, wait. Never mind."

They turned around and walked back, met up with Jimbo who was on shift again at the monorail head, and got a rack to carry them to Theophrastus. On the way, Helene wisely turned the conversation to the subject of getting her suit decorated, and they chatted about designs while they sailed smoothly toward the crater. The green glowing dome of the crater city was as beautiful against the Night sky as before, but Tom was plainly scandalized when Helene suggested using that as an image on her suit.

"Air town? That's them, not us."

"Moon Men use a lot of images from Earth. Since I'm from Earth, why shouldn't I use an image from the Moon? And what else am I going to use, gray dust?"

"Umph," he said ungraciously. The rack canted upward to the Moon Men airlock, and they dismounted and cycled themselves inside.

10: A Story with Padding

They found themselves back on the balcony overlooking the city, their helmets in their hands. Fliers wheeled through the indoor air above the bright-lit boulevards.

"I want to buy some clothes," Helene said. "I don't have anything since my suitcase exploded. What do you do when you come to air town? Do you keep clothes in a locker or something?"

"No, if I'm going to be here for a while I just buy some clothes, then throw them away when I go back home. Come to think of it, I guess it's funny that I can't accept creating garbage when I'm home but it doesn't bother me in air town."

"But isn't that expensive?"

"I'm not here that much, and anyway, if I kept the clothes I'd, you know, have them."

She looked at him quizzically. "I'm trying to picture you in clothes. What style do you wear?"

"Whatever's on sale," he said. "You look beautiful in your suit, but I really want to see you in clothes again, too."

"How long does it take to get a suit painted? A couple of hours? Why don't we leave my suit to be painted and we'll get some dinner?"

"We have to get clothes first, or we won't have anything to wear while your suit gets painted. We have to check into the hotel before that, however, because we'll need to get a technician to get us out of our suits."

"Clothes first, then hotel, then dinner. Which hotel?"

"Do you have a preference?"

"Just that I don't want to go back to the one I was staying in before," she said.

"Okay, the Caravansary, then. I usually go there, and they have artists who will come there so we don't have to bring the suits out." A car arrived for them and they rolled quietly down the zig-zag streets to the crater floor and were carried toward the hotel. The crowds, as Helene had noticed before, were about equally thick at any hour of the day. Every planet in the Ecumene had close to a 24-hour day, and the travelers were all on their own schedules. Most of the businesses ran continuously, and when the smallest mom-and-pop businesses closed at the end of whatever day they observed, others were opening for their own mornings.

Tom stopped them before a clothing shop and they went in, while the car re-entered the street traffic and drove away. Helene's measurements were available from her suit fitting, and Tom's measurements had not, he assured the store clerk, changed since his last purchase.

Helene brought up her full-body image on the display, added undergarments and then tried on a number of different looks. She settled on an ensemble that was currently fashionable on Earth: a smooth sweater of lightweight cotton with a cowl neck in light blue, a long dark blue cotton skirt with a vertical panel of beige, white purse and high-heeled shoes. She added a little necklace with a yellow gem.

Tom, selecting an outfit from the must-go, clearance sale catalog, had something that apparently had been the height of fashion in some nation on Earth II two years ago. His outfit included a broad-brimmed hat, a short ruffled jacket and tights in three shades of green. Helene looked at the image on the display he was using. "Is that really what your body shape is?" she asked.

"I guess so."

"You look pretty muscley. Why would you want to dress up like a cake topper? Here, let me help you out." She chose a white buttoned shirt with fancy cufflinks, brown pleated pants and brown shoes.

"Kind of expensive," Tom complained. "I can only stay away from work for a day or two. Also, it looks a little stodgy."

"I like stodgy. As you ought to know."

"Okay, let's have these delivered to the hotel," he said. They left, and walked two blocks to the Caravansary Hotel, but did not hold hands because their bulky suits would have blocked the sidewalk entirely.

Check-in was accomplished entirely by an electronic conversation between their suits and the hotel computer. A young woman technician led Helene away in one direction to have her suit removed, while a male technician led Tom the other way. Helene stood uncomfortably while the technician unfastened the ring gasket at her waist joint with specialized tools, uncoupled the power, signal, water and other connections, and helped her pull out of the upper half of the suit. She was then even more uncomfortable while the technician hinged opened the bottom half at various junctures and helped her remove appliances intimately connected to her body. The robot cart from the clothes shop arrived and she was able to get dressed. The clothes fit perfectly.

When she reappeared in the hotel lobby, Tom was already there, dressed in the clothes she had picked out for him. He was standing with a young man dressed in a red robe and carrying a large tablet computer. "Helene," Tom said, "this is Henrik Artor. He painted the design for my suit, and for a bunch of other people in my family. I think he's really good. Henrik, this is Helene Friedman."

"It's very nice to meet you, Helene," Henrik said, extending his hand. "Tom, you may remember what I said about that design when I did it for you. I haven't changed my opinion."

"Spices are a good choice for me," Tom said stoutly. "I sell spices."

"My job is to give the client what he wants, but still ..." Henrik said. "We should be grateful you aren't in the business of selling hemorrhoid cream. Helene, what can I paint for you that will be beautiful and represent the real you and won't be a bunch of leaves and piles of powder with labels?"

"I love the way this crater city looks during the Night when we come in on the monorail," Helene said. "Could you do that for me?"

Henrik looked startled. "Helene," he said, "come here and talk with me." He led her a few feet away and said in a low tone, "I'm not a Moon Man but I know how they think. They come here for sex. I presume that's why you are here now?" Helene nodded, her lips tight together. "If I put a picture of this city on your suit," Henrik continued, "the boys are going to look at that and get the message 'I want to get laid.' Let's try to come up with something else, okay?" He led her back to Tom.

"Let's try to come up with something cheerful and pleasant," Henrik said. "Something that really speaks to you. Tom, could we come up with a motif that would work for both you and Helene? Something that would suggest you're a couple?"

"We're only a temporary couple. I'm going back home in a little while," Helene said.

"But of course! When you leave, Tom will no longer look like he's half of a couple because no one else will have a matching design, but you will both have a memento that reminds you of your happy and significant hours together, eh? Now, what do you have in common?"

"Not much, I guess. I'm from the Moon," Tom said slowly. "Helene's from Earth."

"But we all share the same Sun, don't we? Picture a bright, generous, stylized Sun, one design for Helene and one that is similar, but not quite the same, for Tom!" Henrik sketched a couple of hasty designs on his tablet and beamed at them. "You will bring sunshine wherever you go, you will show the world that you are together, Tom will have a fresh look and Helene will be radiant! Radiant!"

Helene smiled and said, "I like it. And Tom, you can always go back to your old design when I'm gone, right?"

Tom looked rebellious for a moment, then relaxed and said, "Okay, okay. It's a deal."

"I will have your suits ready by tomorrow," Henrik said. "Spend the night creating the bond that your suits will symbolize!"

As they walked away, Helene hissed, "If I pick up any speech habits while I'm here, somebody is going to punch me in the nose when I get back home. Does *anybody* here understand the concept of personal space?"

"Oh, Henrik works with Moon Men all the time. I guess he doesn't talk to other people the way he talks to us. Most air-towners will keep theirs and your personal lives to themselves. Seems a little lonely to me, but I'm prejudiced. Let's go get dinner. I know a Moon Man place that isn't just for tourists."

"I think I've had enough meatballs and little chunky things for a while," Helene said. "I mostly went to Earth American restaurants before, but I know they have all kinds, so tell me something that Moon Men don't usually get a chance to eat. Also, Mr. Spicy, not too full of the spices you wouldn't sell to air-towners anyway."

"There's a Nova Terran place where they have stew. Moon Men don't have any good way to eat stew, and it's supposed to be pretty tasty."

"What's in the stew?"

"I have no idea. The whole deal with stew is you're supposed to eat it without asking that question, right? Any ethnic stew is made of what-we-got boiled together with spices."

"Okay, let's be adventurous," Helene said. "Moon Men really don't eat stew?"

"Well, we would have to blenderize it so we could drink it from a liquids bottle. There's not much point."

"You guys are weird."

"But lovable, right?" Tom said.

"Lovable, yes. Still weird, though."

They strolled out of the hotel and down the street. Helene said, "I went to about a dozen provisioning companies here before I met you, and I actually made some pretty good sales. But there are a couple I didn't get to, so I might make an appointment with them while I'm here."

"How about if we spend a day just being together, and then I'll leave you here because I have to work?"

"Okay, I'll just make a couple of sales calls after you go, then follow you. Anyway, yeah, let's be tourists tomorrow. What do they have here to see? I have no interest in casinos."

"There's a zoo," Tom said dubiously.

"That could be fun," Helene said. "What do they have? Elephants or tigers or something?"

"No, big animals cost too much. Aside from farm animals, all they have is a collection of little rodent-things from eight planets. Some of them are kind of interesting. We bring our school kids here because those are the only animals most of them will ever see. They always hate it, by the way."

Helene suddenly peered ahead and said, "Look, that park bench! Is that Gregor and Yeni?"

"Yeah."

"They don't look too good."

"They sure don't. What the hell?"

Yeni was sitting on one end of the bench. Out of her suit, she was a stocky, pretty woman with unstyled blond hair cut short. She was wearing a knee-length dark skirt and silk blouse, she was facing away from Gregor and her cheeks were wet with tears. Gregor was in no better shape. He was tall, well-muscled and looked good in a tunic and shorts, but his face was working and he was facing away as well.

"Gregor? Yeni?" Tom said hesitantly. They both turned to look at Tom and Helene, and Yeni tried a weak smile. "Hi," she said. "Helene, you sure know how to pick clothes. Me, I have no fashion sense at all. I had to let the clerk pick stuff out for me."

"Hey," Gregor said. "Nice to see you."

Tom and Helene looked at each other and came to a wordless agreement. "Gregor," Tom said, "why don't you come with me and we'll get a beer?"

"They don't have any regular beer around here," Gregor said. "I get all urpy if I drink the fizzy stuff."

"Then we'll find something that doesn't fizz," Tom said. "Come on. Yeni, I'll have him back in a while, okay?"

"Okay."

When the men had left, Helene sat next to Yeni. "We can go get a beer, too," she said. "Or chocolate, which I think you deserve a prescription for, or deep-fried something. Or we can just sit here. What do you need, Yeni?"

Yeni looked at her, said nothing and began to cry. Helene held her and said, "I kind of figured that was what you needed. Cry it out, honey. It's okay. Just let it all come up."

"Everybody's looking at me."

"Don't kid yourself. They're looking at this naked tourist bimbo back a way behind you. No, don't turn around. So, the honeymoon's not going so well?"

Yeni wailed even louder. When she had quieted a little, Helene said, "Yeni, let me take a guess about what happened. I had to take care of a friend of mine back in Chicago after *her* honeymoon, so this isn't just a Moon Man thing. Her name is Condell and she's a beautiful black girl from the south side. I met her at work. Her family was in this gorgeous big old church and knew everybody, and they were fairly rich, so when she got married she had like four hundred people attending, she had twelve bridesmaids in lavender silk, she had a wedding gown with a train so long they had four little girls carrying it, she got a ring big enough people were pulling her over all night to look at it. They had a famous band playing at the reception. They had a release of doves. Then they went for a honeymoon at a resort in the islands. They came home four days early and she wound up crying on my couch just like you're doing. Yeni, she's okay with her husband now and you will be too. You get over these things."

Yeni looked at her and said in a very small voice, "Gregor is impotent."

"That happens all the time after a big wedding. It'll pass, it'll pass. Look, the guy's under a lot of pressure. You had this big ceremony, he just pledged the rest of his life, everybody was looking at him. He's known you for a long time, right? But always in a Moon Suit. Now you're naked together and this time he *has* to perform. I suppose Gregor and you have been to air town together before?"

"Twice. He was okay those times."

"Twice, but this time you're tired, a little drunk, all the stimulation from the biggest event of your life has just stopped suddenly and you're in a hotel room surrounded by people who aren't members of your tribe and don't understand you. Yeni, it doesn't mean anything. He'll get his mojo back the next time you come here."

"We haven't had any sex in three days, but it wasn't always because he couldn't get it up. I wasn't getting wet even when he touched me. We went out to a restaurant with food we had never heard of, and got sick all day yesterday," Yeni said. "He yelled at the bartender and I yelled at him and we got into this fight and we both threw up from the food. We tried to go flying and I fell and he laughed at me. Just now we went for a walk and he looked at this woman with her butt hanging out ..."

"The one in the park here?"

Yeni tried to smile. "No, some other tourist slut. They have a lot of them here. Anyway, I told him to stop and he didn't and we had a fight and now we have to go home tomorrow."

"You only had, what, four days for a honeymoon? That doesn't seem long enough."

"It isn't, but our jobs don't give us much paid vacation time," Yeni said.

"What do you do?"

"We're both repair techs for shipboard equipment. I do refrigeration systems, and Gregor does air regeneration. The pay's okay but the benefits aren't much. That's how we met. We work for different companies but we wound up on the same job a bunch of times."

"You and Gregor are going to be okay. Honestly, this will work out."

"I love him," Yeni said, "but ..."

"Stop right there," Helene said. "Yeni, there's always a 'but.' I don't care who he is, it'll be something. He wants sex when he hasn't brushed his teeth, he farts when you're feeling romantic, he has a jackass laugh, something. If you're going to be married, you have to not concentrate on that stuff."

Yeni looked piercingly at her. "Helene, you aren't married on Earth, are you? That wouldn't be kind to Tom."

"No, no, I've never been married. I'm just full of advice. All of it free and all worth what it costs."

"Okay, I'm sorry I doubted you. Thanks for helping."

"I see a guy over there selling ice cream," Helene said. "You want some?"

Yeni considered, then said, "Yes. I'm over being sick. Actually, I want ice cream even if I'm not over being sick. It would still be worth it."

Helene rose and walked over to the pushcart, then discovered that she had no cash and her credit was tied to her Moon suit. Yeni saw what was happening and joined her, paying for two chocolate sundaes with the wave of a ring on her finger. "Tom should have remembered to tell you to get one of these if you're coming to air town," she said.

"Does that count as a wedding ring?" Helene said, smiling. They walked back to the bench.

"No," Yeni said. "It's tied to my own bank account. You know, the only thing we have visually to show we're married is the symbol on our suits. When we're in air, we don't have anything other people can see."

"So you'll do it with interpretive dance, right? When Gregor comes back, you put an arm around his waist, pull him close, look up and give him the

116

smoldering glance. Everybody around you will figure it out. Even Gregor will finally figure it out. I mean, probably."

She giggled. "Okay. Meanwhile, ice cream. This is so good." They ate together in silence for a while.

Presently Tom and Gregor returned. "Hi, boys," Helene said. "You don't look real drunk."

"Hi. Yeah, we mostly just did some manly whining and complaining," Tom said.

Yeni stood and performed her dance: arm around his waist, look up, passionate expression. Gregor caught her subtle hints and kissed her.

"Gregor, Yeni, we're going to finish going out for dinner. You two be good, and we'll see you back in the village, okay?" Tom said tactfully. Yeni hugged Helene one last time and she and Gregor walked away holding hands.

"Thanks for talking Yeni down," Tom said, as they walked toward the Nova Terran restaurant.

"Gregor looked pretty upset, too," Helene said. "I hope we got them fixed up."

"Yeah, he panicked when he couldn't get it up."

"Tom! You can't just pass on stuff like that that somebody tells you in confidence!"

Tom looked at her and smiled. "Who are you talking to? I'm a Moon Man, remember? I know perfectly well Yeni would have told you that because she's a Moon Man too." He paused, then looked pensive. "Actually, that kind of thing is a plague on us, happens all the time. Gregor would have realized that if it had happened to somebody else."

He stopped, looked at Helene and said, "Helene, we *are* strange and we lead unnatural lives and the

117

truth is that we know it. It's so hard for us to arrange time for sex that we get over-wrought and anxious when we finally do it. We have all kinds of sex problems. If you wanted to know about the secret lives of Moon Men, you just got put in the middle. We never talk about it, but I think we all know deep down inside that the way we live our lives isn't a long-term solution." He studied her face.

"Tom," she said seriously, "this is taking me out of my comfort zone, too. I decided I was willing to sleep with you and then I just said so. I've never done that so ... so directly before. It's odd to have so much *process* before we can make love – we have to come here, buy clothes, go through that horrible un-suiting thing, rent a room, not to mention talk about it frankly. It all seems more like a negotiation than a roll in the hay."

They resumed walking. "Thank you for making that effort," Tom said. "Really, I think I understand how much you're sacrificing, and I appreciate it. Here's the restaurant. Let's have romantic stew together."

"What makes stew romantic?" Helene asked.

"You take some out of my bowl and I'll take some out of your bowl. Our eyes will meet and it will be an intimate moment. Have I told you how beautiful you look wearing clothes? Ooh, this is gonna be good." This restaurant was also an outdoor cafe, and they seated themselves and looked over the menu displayed on the tabletop. Helene guessed that the colonists of Nova Terra had come from either exotic places on Earth or from other colony worlds, because none of the dishes had familiar names. The menu showed the ingredients but many of the names were not helpful.

Tom, utterly confident on the subject of food, picked out two different stews for them. Helene looked over the ingredients and said, "This will be exciting, to be eating meat and vegetables from an alien planet."

"People can't eat any plant or animal that evolved on another planet," Tom said, surprised. "Don't they know that on Earth? The proteins are made of the wrong amino acids, totally useless to humans. All of the human food on the planets comes from Earth stock the colonists brought with them. Those alien rodents in the zoo, they have to eat food brought in from their home planets. That's why it's so expensive to keep them."

"This is not Earth food!" Helene said. "Look at this list! I recognize a couple of things like potatoes and turnips but there's no such thing on Earth as a 'nutria.' I presume some biologist coined that name for some kind of alien 'nutritious animal,' right?"

Tom looked down. "Nutria are from Earth."

"Seriously? What are they?"

"They're ... they're good. The meat doesn't have much taste – chefs say that it 'accepts seasoning well.' So it will be spiced Nova Terran style, which I don't know much about but it's supposed to be tasty."

"But what is a nutria?"

"Good meat for a stew. Look, here comes the food now." A serving cart rolled up with steaming bowls, tableware and glasses of a dark red wine. Tom lifted everything to their table and the cart removed itself.

"Do both bowls have nutria?" Helene asked.

"Yours does. Mine is a pork stew, which would be from pigs raised locally. The nutria probably had to be brought from Nova Terra."

"Switch," Helene said.

She exchanged their bowls, then waited while Tom bowed his head for grace. She cautiously tasted the pork stew. "This is good!" she said. "Not quite like any cooking I ever had, but yummy!"

"This is good too. Want a taste?"

"Thank you, no. We'll make our intimate moments some other way. Tom, do you always say grace before meals?"

"Yeah, it's just something my whole family does. You don't have to. What religion is your family?"

"We're non-observant Jews. I mean totally non-observant, no-synagogue-unless-somebody's-kid-has-a-bar-mitzvah, ham-sandwich-eating Jews. Basically nothing, in other words. But your family actually goes to that flat First Baptist Church, don't they? Even when nobody's getting married?"

"We do. But Helene, there's no drama between us on that account, you understand?"

"I do know that, Tom," Helene said, and extended her hands to take his. "You and your family made me welcome without knowing anything about me – well, without knowing anything that the suit didn't report. I appreciate that. It's nice to have that trust."

Tom held her hands and did not let go quickly. "Sure you don't want some of this stew? It's delicious."

"That much trust, we don't have yet. We may never have that much trust, sweetie baby honey darling."

Tom drank some wine and mentioned, "This comes from a winery right here in Theophrastus, and I think they have tasting tours. We could do that."

"Sure. Tom, I'll go wherever you lead me. Even to a casino, although in that case I won't say anything but I will make faces."

When they had finished, they left to walk to the hotel. On the way, Helene said, "Tom, one thing I want to tell you before we get there. I'm wearing a padded bra. I'm not flat-chested or anything, but this isn't all me."

"Okay."

"I just wear pads because I think it makes me look more balanced. I'm a little beamy across the hips, you know?"

"No problem."

"I just wanted you to know ahead of time."

Tom smiled at her. "I'm pretty sure you've made that speech to other guys, haven't you?"

"Well, yes."

"Were any of them jerk enough to complain about it?"

"No, no, they were nice."

"I will be too."

When they reached their room, they embraced and kissed. Tom said, "I have an idea. Please, take off all your clothes except for your bra."

"Wouldn't you like to help me?"

"I think I'm going to need you to help me," he said, abashed.

Helene flashed him a broad grin in sudden understanding. "You're not used to clothes, are you?"

"Um, yeah. I sometimes have trouble with buttons. I'm not going to look real smooth."

"Then I'll just have to unbutton you," she said, and reached forward to begin opening his shirt. She helped him pull off his shirt, then watched while he pulled off his undershirt. "You have hair on your chest! That's a bonus for me." She stroked his chest.

Tom was obliged to sit on the bed to kick off his shoes and remove his pants, not having had much practice in the art of undressing while standing. He watched in rapt appreciation as Helene undressed without flirting or fussiness. She took off all of her clothes except her bra, then stood with her arms out, welcoming. Tom rose to hold her again.

"My skin is touching your skin," he murmured after they kissed again. "You don't have any idea what a wonderful gift you're giving me."

"It's a pleasure for me, too."

"But it's not ... it's not a major life event for you. People who live in air, they can touch each as much as they want. It's different for me."

"Maybe not as different as you think. Tom, this is important. It is."

"Lie down with me."

They tumbled – an odd slow tumble in the low gravity – into the bed. Helene said, "I'll tell you something I like about the Moon. You can lie right on top of me and I don't get squashed!"

Tom smiled but rolled off of her anyway and lay propped up on one elbow. They kissed for a long while, then Tom said, "Now I want some permission."

"Well, of course, dear."

"Oh. Thank you, but I meant I want you to take my hand in your hands, and guide it to your bra. Now tell me I have your permission to touch your pads."

"Tom, of course you can touch my pads," she said, positioning his hand. "But why?"

"Sex is more mental than physical, and it's visual too. Look where my hand is."

Helene looked. Tom said, "Have you ever let a man touch your pads?"

She caught on to his game, and said, "Look where your hand is. Tom, I have never let a man touch me there. You're the first."

"Your pads are warm because they're right next to your skin, and they smell like you, and you're a little self-conscious about them, which makes you a little vulnerable, doesn't it? If anyone had ever criticized you about your pads, you'd be hurt, right? But you let me touch them. You told me I could, and I'm very honored."

Helene kissed him, and pressed his hand down on her bra. "I've always been shy about letting a man know I have pads. If any man had tried to touch my pads without permission, I would have slapped him. But you can do it. I want you to keep doing it."

"It gets better. I think we can make a new erogenous zone for you, one other women don't have." Tom stroked her bra cup gently and said, "Feel the sensation?"

"They're just foam."

"Use your erotic imagination."

"Tom," Helene said in a small voice, "you're right. I can feel them responding. They're getting warm and full and rising into your hand. My pads like you. I think you've hypnotized me." She breathed deeply, and her chest rose.

"I can feel them swelling up. I can kiss them." Tom kissed one bra cup, then the other.

Helene groaned and arched her back. "Tom! I actually did feel that! It's like ... I don't know what it's like. Oh my god, kiss my pads again and this time let me watch."

Tom kissed her bra cups again, and Helene watched wide-eyed. She rolled on top of him. They held each other and she said, "I know it's just me being suggestible, but you actually did give me a new erogenous zone. Damn, you're good. Have you done that trick with other women?"

"I never thought of that before. You bring out a side of me I didn't know I had."

"Tom," she whispered, "kiss me anywhere. Kiss me everywhere. But don't let my poor little paddies get lonely."

Tom rolled her down to the bed again and moved his head down to kiss her body. Anywhere and everywhere.

*   *   *

The light outside was unchanged, but the room lights came up on the "morning" schedule they had specified as part of checking in. After more caresses and kisses, Helene rose, still wearing her bra, and began to dress. Tom said, "I still haven't actually seen your breasts."

She grinned. "They're a little small, but *super* cute and attractive. Really, they're awesome. If you ever see them, you'll faint from the rush of blood to your ... from the rush of blood."

"If?" he said, alarmed.

"I've decided they're so good, I'm going to keep them in reserve. I'm going to save them for a special treat for the fellow who marries me."

"Are you trying to manipulate me?"

"Of course I am! Judging from your face, it's working, too," Helene said. "I am a sales professional. I know some techniques to close a deal." She finished dressing and turned to face him. She took a deep breath and said, "Do you like what you see?"

"Oh, my god."

"Good. Hold that thought. In fact, obsess about that thought. Meanwhile, take me out for breakfast."

"Helene, don't do this to me ..."

"Tom, I'm just messing with you! Of course I'll give you anything I've got. But look, doing anything on this dumb one-sixth of a planet requires planning out our steps. Step Two is to order us another set of clothes, Step Three is to come back here for a shower once we have clean clothes to change into, and I think you can guess what Step Four is going to be. But Step *One* is to get breakfast because I'm starving."

"We did burn up a bunch of calories last night," Tom said.

"I know, right? Do you think anybody here can make those blueberry pierogies? Those were really good."

"Not like Aunt Carletta. You'll have to settle for lesser food."

Tom dressed himself but got his shirt buttons one-off the first time he tried, and had to be helped by Helene. Eventually they made it out the door.

11: My Heart is Probably Stronger Than Yours

After getting a good breakfast, ordering clothes, showering and achieving Step Four more than once, Helene and Tom were able to get a car out to Tumblewater Creek Winery in the farm country on the east side of Theophrastus Crater. They rode past half a kilometer of grapevines grown by aeroponics, suspended on wires below bright lamps. The vines were tended by particularly scary-looking robots, boxes riding on rails between the rows with many busy metal arms reaching up to water, fertilize, pollinate and harvest the grapes on both sides. The processing machinery and fermenting tanks were out in the open, in the middle of the vineyard.

The winery of course had no creek, tumbling or otherwise, but did have a decorative pond adjoining the winery building, a pseudo-Italian cottage of timber and stucco. Somewhat to her surprise, they were greeted by a human hostess, a young woman wearing a peasant dress, who led them to a table by the pond. As they sat, a man and woman flew overhead, landed neatly on the ground on the far side of the pond and pulled off their wings and harnesses. The hostess also found a table for them.

Helene still had no way to spend money, so Tom allowed the tabletop to look at the irises of his eyes,

126

and ordered a light lunch of cold dishes and tasting flights of red and white wines. The hostess seemed to be the only human employee; the food and wine were delivered by a robot cart. "I don't drink wine much," Helene said. "Back home, I mean. The truth is, I don't even know what good wine is supposed to taste like. When I have to bring wine to a party or something I just buy what's expensive."

"Now that you mention it," Tom said, "I'm not sure I know what bad wine tastes like. My cousin Avera orders all the wine for the Easterday family, and everybody says she's a real expert. I know we buy from this winery once in a while, but I've never had any wine that wasn't picked out by Avera. I wonder what they'd say if I asked for their cheap, grade-B, inferior wine? I'm sure they must have some, and I'd be curious to try it."

"You're not an expert on wine? I thought you were the all-purpose food guru?"

"Certainly I'm an expert." Tom lifted one small goblet of red wine with an elaborate gesture, sipped a little with audible slurping noises and said, "Ah, excellent! A bright berry flavor with an undertone of cheeseburger, and nuances of oak, licorice, maple syrup and oleomargarine."

"Okay," Helene said, smiling, "you're a wine guy, too. A man of many talents."

"Despite the fact that I talk about food all the time," Tom said, "the truth is I don't think anybody can actually talk well about food or wine. When you talk about wine, it always sounds like some kind of mutant fruit punch. I can taste that some wines are particularly good with certain foods, but I can't actually say why. That doesn't stop me from answering when somebody asks why I chose that wine, of course."

They ate for a while. Tom said, "I need some more permission. Can I look into your eyes now without you snapping at me?" Helene smiled, looked down a moment, then lifted her face to look back at him.

When he was not looking at Helene, Tom's eyes went to the pond. It was shallow, lined with plastic and boasted flowering lily pads and a few small goldfish. At one point the hostess happened to walk by, and Tom waved her over. "Excuse me," he said, "but I've never seen open water like that on the Moon. Is that really plain water?"

"Not quite," she said. "You couldn't drink it or anything. We have to add chemicals to keep algae from growing in it. We also put in plant food, fish food and detergent. We forgot the detergent one time and all around the edge, the surface tension was rolling the water up into little balls. It looked pretty strange."

"Thank you," he said, and the hostess walked away. To Helene he said, "I see ponds and oceans and things in movies all the time, but you know, that's the first one I've ever seen in real life. It's kind of disturbing. I mean, there's no cover. I keep thinking the water should dry up or boil or something."

"Tom, this is some decorator's imitation of a pond. Real ponds are completely different, believe me."

"I suppose so."

Helene was silent for a while, then could not restrain herself from speaking. "Tom," she said in a tight voice, "look, I don't want to criticize your whole world, but *nothing* on the Moon is real. This winery is a stage setting in front of a factory, the pond has a plastic bottom, Theophrastus looks sort of like a real city but it's unnaturally clean and most of the population is tourists and transients. I know you can't ever come to Earth but I wish I could show it to you."

"Why can't I come to Earth?"

"Because you live in one-sixth gravity and your heart is weakened?"

Tom smiled. "That's for air-towners. Me, I've spent my entire life living and working in a Moon suit that weighs four times my body weight. Every time I move my arms or legs, there's a little resistance which gives me exercise. My heart is probably stronger than yours. I could go to Earth if I wanted to. In fact, it's something I always wanted to do before I get old. I'd like to see Paris."

Helene sat for a moment, toying with her food. She said quietly, "All this time, I've been thinking you could never come to Earth, and I could never stay here because if I did I couldn't go home. Now I have to re-think that."

"All of a sudden I'm not as unavailable as you thought I was," Tom said. He reached across the table for her hands, and said, "Helene, we've had a wonderful three days and I will always be grateful for what you've given me, but nobody's talking about marriage and you're not under any pressure from me or anybody else, okay? It's been splendid but it will end and we both know that. I can accept it and you should, too."

"I guess I was talking about marriage this morning," Helene said.

"Well, yes, but then you gave away your very powerful bargaining chip. Chips."

"Yes, I did."

"And if I haven't said so, they were everything you promised."

She put a finger on his lips. "Thank you, but be serious with me for a moment. Tom, I want to take you to Earth and show you ... I don't know, everything. Everything real and natural, all the places where human beings are *supposed* to be. But I don't want you to stay because I don't want to think I made you give up your whole world, and your family and friends and work. I don't want you to come for a visit because then you'd have to go away again. I don't want to live here and I don't want to come back for a visit because then I'd have to go away. I don't know what I want but I'm sure I can't get it. I love you."

"It's too early to say that, and you can hurt me by saying that."

"You're right. I didn't say it."

"And I didn't hear it. Meanwhile, this wine may not be real but it's a very credible fake, so why don't you knock back a couple or six glasses, and then we'll go see something else here in fabulous Theophrastus Crater. Maybe the zoo."

"I find, after thinking it over," Helene said, "that I can live without seeing the Rodents of Eight Planets."

"The tabletop is tied into the network," Tom said. "Let me bring up pictures of the animals in the zoo. Some of them are pretty strange and interesting." Helene moved her plate aside and watched as the menu was replaced with pictures of various small brown animals. She swiped from one to another, then stopped.

"That? That's a nutria? From Earth?" she asked.

"Um, yes."

"You are in so much trouble, buster."

"You didn't even taste that stew, and it was good. Okay, the zoo is out. Back in town they have live music concerts, plays, magicians, prize fights, all kinds of stuff to make sure travelers changing ships don't leave with any money in their accounts. I'm sure we can find something."

"Dear Tom, we don't have to find anything particular to amuse ourselves."

"We can't go back to the hotel room for a while. My heart is strong but it's not *that* strong, Miss Physicality. They sell bottles of wine over by the building there. Do we want to buy one to take with us?"

Helene glanced over at the building. "I'm surprised they have glass bottles here. I mean, they're so heavy."

"Glass is something we cook out of the dust, during the Day, along with metal, oxygen and helium-3," Tom said. "It's so cheap it's almost free. But you'd have to be crazy to pay the freight to carry glass bottles to or from the Moon. If we get a bottle, we'll just turn it in at the hotel when we've drunk it and they'll send it back here to be washed and reused."

"I don't think this wine is all that exciting anyway," Helene said. "Let's just go."

They called for a car, then rode back through the same vineyard lane toward the urban part of the crater. "Tom, would you rather just go get our suits and go back outside? You're looking like you've had enough air town," Helene said.

"The main amusement back in the village is gossiping," Tom said. "Sports, dancing, whatever you can watch inside your helmet, and church services, but mostly gossiping. It won't kill me to stay in air town a while longer, and I should quit being a priss about it anyway."

A flock of a dozen teenagers with wing harnesses happened to pass overhead. They were laughing and talking loudly to each other. Helene glanced up and said, "I certainly hope birds like that don't poop when they fly."

"Birds just crap while they're flying?" Tom asked. "I always thought they had nests or something."

Helene could not suppress a snort. "Tom," she asked, "how much biology did they teach you?"

He thought a moment. "One required class in high school, plus a class on food handling, which had some stuff on plants and animals."

"I thought you went to college."

"There's only one college on the Moon for Moon Men, and it's a two-year technical school over in Mare Nectaris," Tom said. "That's where I know Gregor from. He was in Systems Tech, I was in Business. But there wasn't any biology, although they did have some science classes."

"You're kind of amazing, you know that? Anyway, yes, on Earth birds just let fly wherever they happen to be. Every once in a while, some lands on you. We learn to cope with it."

"Yuck. I never saw that in a movie or anything."

"Tom, could we try to go flying?"

Tom looked at her. "It's harder than it looks. Unless you're in pretty good athletic shape, flapping those wings really takes it out of you. Also, teenagers are skinnier than you and me. Tell you what, though. See that thing in the sky over there?" He pointed.

"The delta wing?"

"Right. It's kind of a flying bicycle. I know where we can rent a couple of those. They're ... um, they're not cool, you understand. Mostly they're for old people. They have electric propellers and they don't go fast, and you can't do tricks or anything. In fact, the bike has a controller that won't let you get too close to any buildings or do anything dangerous. But they are easy and you get to fly, which is kind of fun."

"Let's do that. We've had plenty of exercise for the day anyway."

The vineyards and farms gave way to casinos and beer halls. The car took them through the city and climbed switchback roads to a place far up on the crater wall, almost at the seam where the crater rock met the dome. When they stepped out in front of "Free As A Bird Flight Gear Rental: Don't Be a Chicken – You Can Fly!" they were as high above the crater floor as the top stories of the hotels and casinos. The salesman was a young man wearing a conical hat which apparently was fashionable on whatever planet formed his odd accent. His expression carefully did not change when Tom explained what they wanted. He led them past racks of harness wings decorated with flame designs, racing stripes, feather designs or what appeared to be actual feathers. At the side of their open-air office were several ungainly one-person flying bicycles, none of which had flame designs.

They had triangular Rogallo wings, with a three-wheeled cab suspended below that had both a big propeller driven by a bicycle crank, and supplementary wings terminated in smaller, electric propellers. A smooth apron of open ground sloped downward before them, so that the flyer could build up to air speed. Tom climbed into one saddle by himself, while the salesman helped Helene into hers, brushing her body unnecessarily as he strapped her in.

"Just keep the propeller moving and you'll be fine," he said. "Tilt this bar to turn left or right, push it forward to go down, pull it to go up. When you're ready to quit, don't try to come back here to land — that's too difficult. Just land wherever you won't hit anybody, then drop the bike in any place where it's not blocking traffic. Your rental fee includes pick-up service. If you get in trouble, the bike controller will take over and land you safely. Got it?" Helene nodded. "Okay, then fly like a bird!" The salesman released the brakes and pushed her downslope.

Helene pedaled furiously, the big propeller spun, and she was able to lift off the ground and clear the thickly-padded barrier at the lower end of the launch apron. She lurched into the air, slewed left and right, then was able to climb toward the dome. The city of Theophrastus Crater spread below her.

"How you doin'?" Tom yelled. He was flying as near as his bike controller would allow, more stable than Helene.

"Okay! Whee! This is fun!" she hollered.

"Head for Main Street!" he shouted, pointing to the central street most of the tallest buildings were on.

Presently Helene discovered, by watching a few other flying bikes go by ridden by gray-haired pilots, that it didn't actually make much difference whether she pedaled hard or not. The electric propellers were doing most of the work. She followed Tom's lead and they swooped between the casinos and hotels, above the thickly populated sidewalks. She spotted one amusement place featuring trampolines that allowed the jumpers to reach amazing heights, and resolved to try that when she had the opportunity.

Conversation was exhausting, so Tom and Helene rode without shouting to each other. They sailed over streets, circled some of the giant trees in the parks, found themselves once again over the farm country.

There was one annoyance. Manual fliers, either teenagers or adults who were obviously proud of their fitness, buzzed her and Tom repeatedly. They flew too close in front of her, overtook her from behind, did spins and loops in the air ahead while grinning at her condescendingly. When Helene pedaled harder, she went slightly faster. When she slacked off, the bike kept flying. Finally she just resolved to ignore the other fliers.

One woman returned several times, however. She was blonde, skinny, perhaps in her early thirties.

She passed in front of Helene and looked sharply at her face, then banked and sailed away. When Tom and Helene neared the far crater wall and began a wide, easy turn back toward the city, she was there again, staring at Helene. Again she came close, looked and was gone with powerful strokes of her wings.

Helene pointed to her as she receded after one approach. Tom looked, then lifted his arms to shrug. Helene noted that it did not particularly seem to bother the bicycle that his hands were off the control bar.

Theophrastus Crater was nine kilometers in diameter. Helene thought of it as a circle about 40 blocks across; in Chicago terms, a neighborhood from downtown on the east to Pulaski Avenue on the west, from Fullerton on the north to Cermak on the south. It was quite large enough to have a small but lively city, two villages (although one of them appeared to be a quaint rustic tourist trap rather than a place where anybody actually lived), farms and parks. Industry was largely an outside activity, taking advantage of the Daytime sunlight and vacuum. Most of the residents, and businesses that did not directly cater to travelers, lived in buildings on the crater wall.

They flew past the crater walls, where people ate at cafe tables. Unlike the cafes in the tourist areas, the tables where locals sat had umbrellas and awnings. Helene suddenly understood, after trying to wave to people without response, that the awnings were there so that the residents did not have to look at the cruising tourists.

The blonde woman passed her again, looked at her face, then tilted away.

Finally even the modest effort of pedaling the bike added up, and Helene waved for Tom to land. They happened to be near the tourist village, so they landed on the outskirts, taking a few clumsy bounces, then took off their seat belts and climbed out. Both were walking a little stiffly. They embraced, then pulled the bikes to the side of the road they had landed on, and walked into "town."

It turned out to be called "Little Earth," and was full of restaurants and bars. One part was European, vaguely suggesting some medieval town in Germany. Another part attempted to look like old China, with buildings crowded along alleys called hutongs. They finally settled on a theme-park version of the American old west, with wooden buildings faced with hitching posts. There were a few full-size plastic horses added for decoration. The buildings were all false-fronts concealing automated kitchens, while diners sat as usual at "outdoor" tables. Inevitably, the restaurants were steak houses.

"Definitely here," Tom said. "You understand, I get European little sausages and meatballs all the time, and lots of Chinese food, but getting steak cut up for a sixpack isn't the same thing as getting a good sizzling steak you can slice yourself with a knife. Also, they have mashed potatoes with gravy, which is birthday dinner food for a Moon Man. Not like Mama's home cooking, you know?"

"Have we really reached some kind of limit on your enthusiasm for six-bite cuisine?" Helene asked, as they neared a table. She was momentarily nonplussed when Tom pulled back a chair to seat her, having not encountered that custom often. But she allowed herself to be seated, said her thanks, and waited for Tom to seat himself. The weathered wood of the table was an illusion: the surface faded to present the menu.

"I guess we have," Tom said. "Forgive me for not being consistent?"

"Anytime," she said. "Tom, I hate to ask you to pay for this. These steaks are pretty expensive."

"Some of them undoubtedly were shipped by your company from Earth, since the cow union apparently doesn't allow cows to work on the Moon, or something," he said. "It's okay. When we get a chance, we can go to the bank and get set up for you to pay outside of your suit, and then I'll make you take me out."

"It's a date." They settled on steaks, potatoes, green beans and a red wine, and waited for the serving cart to arrive.

A voice from the sky screamed, "Bitch! You're the one who tried to take my husband!"

They looked up. The blonde woman Helene had seen was plummeting down toward them in a hawk stoop, heels first, her wings together over her head. She apparently had flown straight down to give herself speed, because she crashed into the table much faster than gravity would have propelled her. The table tipped and knocked Helene painfully to the ground. The table rolled away as the flying woman fell and scrambled to her feet. She stripped off her wings and tossed them to the ground, then advanced on Helene with fury in her face.

"You thought you could fuck my husband and I wouldn't find out about it, slut? You're not smart enough for that!" Tom tackled her to the ground. At the same moment, a fast police car pulled up with two yellow-uniformed police. They jumped from the car and grabbed the woman as she lunged for Helene, still screaming. Tom stood back as the two policemen gripped her and pulled her back.

"Did you know she was going to do that?" Tom asked the police. "How did you get here so fast? Who is she?"

"Don't know yet," the male officer said. "We just happened to be in the area, and the air traffic system gave us a flash somebody was doing an unsafe landing here. But I think we'd better hold on to her for a while." He turned to Helene, and asked, "Ma'am, are you okay?"

"Yes, yes, I'm fine. I'm good." Helene scrambled to her feet. Her skirt was ripped.

"Is this woman someone you know?"

"I've never met her. But I guess maybe I do know. I think she's married to a guy named Jacob Hibarger."

"I'm his wife!" the woman shouted. "She's not! Let me go!" The two police put her in handcuffs.

The woman officer went up to Helene and pulled out a device to scan her eyes. "Helene Friedman, Earth?" she asked. Helene nodded. "Okay, if you're not hurt then we'll take this one in. You won't be permitted to leave the city until we've cleared this case, all right? Take this card and call us to find out what your situation is." Helene nodded again.

In a few moments, the police had strapped the blonde down in their car and driven away. Tom picked up the table again as the serving cart pulled up with their food. Other diners at the restaurant, who had been staring at them, turned their faces away again.

Tom helped Helene back into her seat. "Somebody from your past?" he asked.

"Four days ago."

12: Gossip, and Something to Gossip About

Tom lifted their dinners from the serving cart to the table, looked down to say a silent grace, then applied himself to his steak. He said nothing for a long while, and then only remarked, "This is good."

"Tom ..." Helene said, and stopped.

"Helene, you don't have to explain anything to me. Four days ago was before you met me. As far as I'm concerned, that's on the other side of a door."

"I want to talk."

"I want you to eat some of this excellent steak first," Tom said. "Also, mashed potatoes. Also, don't talk with your mouth full. I'll still be here, but if you let this dinner get cold, as a fanatic foodie I'm going to be offended."

Helene smiled a little and asked, "Do I have to eat my beans before I can confess?"

"No, I'll give you a dispensation on the beans. Seriously, right now I want to concentrate on eating a fine steak dinner with a beautiful woman. If you still want to turn on the soap opera afterward, I'll listen then. Meanwhile, is this a great steak or what?"

Helene cut off a slice, chewed it thoughtfully and said, "It's good. I've had better steak back home, but we have a lot more steak houses than you have here and anyway those cost more. For the price, this is prime."

"Ooh, so now you're going to undercut me as Mr. Gourmet? That's a low blow. That gets me right in my manhood."

Helene said, "I'm sorry. I ... have some disadvantages as a girlfriend, I know."

"Joke, joke! Helene, relax, it's okay. Anyway, here's our Couples Rule: if you disagree with me about food, you're wrong. If you disagree with me on any other subject, you're right and I'm wrong, okay? If we hold to that, we've got no problems."

"I submit meekly," Helene said.

When they had finished their food, Helene said, "I have been on the Moon for ten days, now. We have existing customers here in Theophrastus, so I had a bunch of appointments lined up with them and I was working through the list. I was able to get some pretty good orders, actually. Then I went to a company called Rimbold Provisions, which is one of our biggest accounts, and I met a guy named Jacob Hibarger. He gave me a big order, we went out to dinner and we wound up spending the night in my hotel room. I didn't know he was married."

"Did you ask him?"

"As a matter of fact, no." Helene looked Tom in the eye. "Tom, I'm not like that usually. I'm not. But this was going to be my adventure, I'm like 400,000

141

kilometers from home, I knew I was never coming back here and he was kind of hot. You know, for a guy I figured I was never going to see again, anyway."

"So what happened after that?"

"Turns out that his wife is the daughter of the Rimbold who founded the company. Yeah, he's a gold-digger in addition to his other charms. Daddy found out, called my company back on Earth and canceled all their orders. Monday when I went to the wedding with you, I hadn't heard about the fuss and I still thought maybe I'd have dinner again with the guy that night. When I got to the Moon suit place, I found out I'd been fired and kicked out of my hotel. And then you became my friend."

"Not a very exciting story," Tom said. "You wouldn't be the first person who had a little fling on a business trip, that didn't end well. I guess you should have asked the bastard if he was married but he probably would have lied anyway. Helene, *nothing happened*. I mean, as far as you and me. You were single, you thought he was single, you're allowed to go to a room with him if you want. If you want me to, I'll go punch the guy in the nose for you, but otherwise we don't have an issue."

"It wouldn't have happened to a Moon Man woman."

Tom smiled ruefully. "Well, not by surprise, anyway. First of all, if a Moon Man woman winds up in air town without her suit, meets a guy and doesn't tell him that, she's on the prowl. Second, if he knows she's a Moon Man, then he knows it's going to be a one night stand, and if he doesn't know it, she does. And third, there wouldn't be any automatic record when she's out of her suit, but being the people we are, the first thing she'd do when she got back to the village would be to tell all her girlfriends. That would put the story on record and then everybody would know it."

"What in the world do you people gossip about if you already know everything?"

"We re-hash the good parts. Helene, we can't possibly hide any aspect of our lives from each other so we don't even try. We know, in a way I don't think anybody else does, that people lead messy, sexual, unplanned lives with lots of mistakes. We learn not to be judgmental because that's how we *have* to be."

"You're not judging me?"

"Of course not."

Helene was silent for a long time. Finally she said, "Let's go back to the hotel. I suppose the police will know where to find us."

They summoned a car and rode back to the hotel without speaking. Helene led them to the storage room where their suits were. Both suits had been nicely painted in similar "sun" designs. She said, "Tom, I'm going to get the technician to get me suited back up. You don't have to if you don't want to, but I feel the need to have that suit around me now. You were right, I got used to it pretty quickly."

Tom called for a male technician. They were escorted to separate rooms and re-suited. When they met again in the hotel lobby, Helene went to the desk and rented a storage locker for her clothes, then arranged through the concierge to purchase a cheap suitcase for her journey home. Tom watched from a distance. When she took the elevator to their room, she used up so much space that he was obliged to wait for the next car.

Presently they were back in the room together, but in Moon suits with their helmets off. Helene sat on the floor, already better practiced at that procedure, and Tom sat facing her. Helene looked into her helmet and spoke to the suit, then had a phone conversation with someone. "Okay," she said to Tom, "the cops say I can go. They're going to charge the Hibarger woman with making that landing but let her go otherwise. I get a feeling what she really wanted was to keep her husband in anxiety for three days so she could forgive him and have wild apology sex. They're probably going at it right now."

"What do you want to do now?"

"I want to sit here for a few minutes, for one thing."

Tom sat with her for a while, then glanced into his helmet and said, "Helene, I can see you're upset."

"Shut up!" she yelled, then said in a lower tone, "Yes, I'm upset. I'm sorry I yelled at you. But Tom, we are starting a new relationship rule here and now. From now on, you know *nothing* about me except what you can see with your eyes and what *I* tell *you* about myself. Got it? If you ever again look at even one of those 38 data points from my suit, I swear to God I will never talk to you again. Say yes and don't say one other goddam word."

"Yes," Tom said.

"Let's go home."

Helene re-attached her helmet even before she reached the elevator. They took a car up to the rim airlock. Tom donned his helmet at that point, they cycled through and rode the monorail back to the village. As they drew near, Helene could see players dancing for a game of pitch and toss, presumably a different shift. Ships rose and landed in Sinus Amoris field. They landed behind the terminal building and walked into the village.

Tom said, "You probably want to go to bed without talking to anybody, right? I didn't look at your suit data, I'm just guessing. It's been a long day."

"Yeah."

"Here, stop a moment." Tom put his interface finger up to the port on her arm and said "I'm going to raise the 'Do Not Disturb' flag on your suit. That means nobody will talk to you and nobody can see your suit data. It stays in place until you try to talk to somebody else, then it will be relaxed automatically."

"That woman Oksana said the suit won't take an order like that."

"Oksana is not a Moon Man. She thinks she knows all about us but she doesn't. All of us need to raise that flag once in a while. But Helene, if you leave it on too long people are going to worry about you. I'm going to worry about you."

"Put that flag up for me, Tom, and thanks. I'll see you in the morning. Right now I need vacuum and the Night sky and not to have to talk to anybody."

"Okay. Don't say anything else or you'll break the spell, or at least, take down the Do Not Disturb flag."

They walked into the village. Helene went to her sleeping position in the Easterday compound, plugged herself into the post and sat down to sleep. No one else looked at her face; the social light inside her helmet that would have illuminated her face was dark. She looked up at the stars, then slept.

13: Helene Makes Her Signature Move

Sinus Amoris village did not have restaurants as such, but anybody could walk up to another family's food carts and ask to buy whatever they were having at the non-family price. When she awoke, Helene rose and left the Easterday area without speaking to anyone, then found the Campbell family at their shift's supper time, eating a dinner called *Sweetness Yields to a Sentimental Taste*. Her "Do Not Disturb" flag was still up and her face dark; they politely allowed an automatic purchase arranged between her suit and theirs without any human conversation, and she walked away with three six-packs of a meal based on dumplings filled with meat she could not identify, balls of mixed vegetables and sweet buns. It was delicious, but she ate it without much attention as she walked toward the landing field.

At a word to her suit, she set up an appointment with the ship's chandler Susanna had recommended to her. The appointment was for an hour hence. When she arrived at the edge of the field, she sat on the ground, eating her food and looking up into the Night sky. Two spherical ships landed and three took off during the time she was watching, all of them in cradles with Moon Man harbor pilots. Buses came and went at the passenger terminal, and Moon Man crews supervised robots loading and unloading cargo. Helene watched the bustle without moving.

When the time came, she rose, stowed the empty sixpacks in a compartment in her backpack the suit had to locate for her, and waited while little mechanical arms washed her face. On a whim, wishing to look like other Moon Men women, she also allowed the suit to apply makeup to her face, murmuring instructions while the manipulators pulled up cosmetics from some source hidden inside the trunk of her suit. Finally she walked up to the offices of Quiboon Supply, which apparently employed both Moon Men in an empty square at one side, and air-towner employees in a pressurized building. Jacque Weatherall, the man Susanna had sent him to see, was a Moon Man waiting in front of the building.

Helene walked up to him. He looked at her, waited silently, then finally scribbled on a tablet computer and held it up in front of her. "YOU HAVE TO TALK TO ME FIRST," he had written.

"Oh, hi!" Helene said. "I'm sorry. Can you hear me now? Jacque Weatherall?" The social light inside her helmet went on.

"Yes, I am," Weatherall said. "Susanna told me you'd be coming, and I guess you're not too familiar with our customs, eh? Unless I touch to your interface port and force it, you have to speak first to take down a Do Not Disturb flag."

"Oh, yeah, they told me that."

"Let me just tell you some things that Moon Men already know. Politeness requires that I can't look at any of your history now unless you tell your suit to release your records. But if you don't release your records, that kind of implies to us that you're not trustworthy. I won't criticize you for it, but other people who don't know that you're from Earth will be a little dubious about you."

"Suit, release all my information," Helene said quietly. Jacque considered the data in his helmet for a while and then said, "Okay, nothing that I need to worry about for a business transaction. How are we going to do this?"

"I've given up hoping the company will rehire me, at least until I get back home. But if you give me an order, I'll send it in. I'm sure they'll fulfill it and they will probably pay me a free-lance commission, which isn't as much as I would make regularly but it would be nice to have."

"Good enough. I need some items. How much leeway does your company give salesmen to dicker on orders?" Jacque asked.

Helene smiled. "You can't expect me to tell you that. You're the customer. But I will say I can work with you a little bit."

"Helene, you're with the Moon Men now. I *do* expect you to tell me that, and honestly. We don't keep secrets from each other, even for a business deal."

"Six percent," Helene said after a moment. "They won't accept an order with a discount bigger than that."

"Looking at your price sheet, we don't even have to go that deep," Jacque said. "Four and a half percent puts you a little bit below what I'm paying for meat and a full percent under what I usually have to pay for grains and greens. How about four and a half off? Will the company still pay you a commission at that rate?"

"Yeah, yeah, that will work," Helene said. "But shouldn't we ... I mean, kick this around and negotiate a while?"

"Moon Men don't do that to each other." Jacque mumbled to his suit in quick-speak for a while, and a document ordering two metric tons of beef, shrimp, tuna and specialty meats appeared in Helene's display, along with an order for several tons of wheat and corn. He had also ordered soy sauce, barbecue sauce and other condiments that were inconvenient to prepare locally, in hundred-liter lots.

"Thank you!" Helene said. "That ... that seems like a lot."

"Space ships are like cruise ships on Earth," Jacque said. "Gobble, gobble, gobble. We supply ships in two other ports beside this one, so we'll use that much up before next sunset. If it's good, and you can hold that price, I can order that much or more every month."

"Jacque, thank you for the company and thank you for *me*, personally. I can't tell you how much this means to me. I've always been proud of my ability to negotiate a hard deal but it hasn't worked so well this trip. Getting an easy deal, it's nice."

"I'd rather buy from a Moon Man than a mouth-breather any day," Jacque said. "I know you're not really a Moon Man but you came to me in a suit and let me see your data, and that makes me comfortable." He hesitated, then said "Helene? I don't want to say anything very personal, but you did let me look at your record and I have some advice. I think you need to go talk to the women in the village. You've met some of them, right?"

Helene said, "I will never get used to this. Yes, I have met a few women. They were nice to me but it's not like any of them are close friends."

"You still don't understand Moon Men. You don't need to be close friends to have close conversations around here."

Helene smiled. "I know women like that back home. Never met a man who understood it, though."

"Yeah, we're a little weird that way. Anyway, that's my advice. Let me know if there's any difficulty fulfilling that order, okay?"

"Sure thing. Thanks again!"

Helene walked back into the village and found Gloria Beacon at the food cart, along with another woman and a man she didn't know. "Hi, Helene," Gloria said. "It's my day to cook."

"Hi, Gloria. Is Tom around?"

"I'll have to show you how to get the location of any Moon Man. But no, Tom's not here. We just packed him off to go to his spice shop. He was mooning around and when we got a look at his numbers and you took down your Do Not Disturb flag, we knew we had to get him out of the way. You got him pretty worked up, girl."

"Didn't seem that way to me. I thought he was damn calm."

"No. Anyway, you're in time for lunch. We're making *A Taste of Shadow in the Sunshine*, with my own special spice blend. It's got ..."

"I don't need to know," Helene said. "I'm sure it will be delicious."

Gloria grinned. "Let me school you a little in Moon manners. When a cook wants to talk about food, you don't get to not listen."

"I'll remember that. Tell me about whatever it was you just said."

"The heart of it is seasoned lamb sausage packed into mushroom caps," Gloria began, and continued talking for several minutes, her hands busy in the food cart, while other members of the Easterday family drifted in and chatted with each other until the food was ready. Susanna showed up and appeared ready to launch into a conversation but Gloria said, "Hold on to that, Susanna. Let us finish eating. I want to get in on this."

Most of the Easterdays were on shift at the field. One man, identified in Helene's display as Tom's cousin Enrique, showed up with a car and collected two dozen packages of sixpacks to be delivered on-site.

Helene sat on the ground with the men and women of the family whose jobs allowed them to eat lunch together. She ate her meal thoughtfully, trying to understand the gastronomical logic that informed the sequence of tastes. Once she mentioned this, everyone else tried to explain it to her. When they had different opinions, they tried to explain the correct theory to each other. Helene did not have to talk much to keep the conversation going.

The eighteenth and last bite was a ball of dense chocolate cake with fruit compote in the middle. Everyone was effusive with praise for Gloria and other cooks. The beverage afterward was spiced chai, and Helene sipped it from the container fixed to her helmet and listened to the conversation around her. Eventually Gloria finished cleaning her food cart, with water that was carefully stored for recycling, and came over to sit by Susanna and Helene. Most of the others rose to go back to work.

"I don't want it to sound like I'm sending you away," Helene said, "but don't you have to go work?"

"I'm a bookkeeper. I work for six little companies over at the field, but I don't have to go in on any particular schedule," Susanna said.

"And I'm supercargo whenever my company has to load up a ship," Gloria said. "But we don't happen to have anything going out until tonight, which is why I signed up for kitchen duty. I'll probably wind up working late, but I'm off right now. Helene, Tom thinks you're having a temporary fling with him because you actually are, aren't you? You know you're going back to Earth."

Helene winced, then sighed. "I am *so* not a real Moon Man. It gives me whiplash every time you suddenly dive off the high board into the deep end like that."

"I don't understand," Gloria said.

"Oh. I guess it's an Earth thing. We have swimming pools full of water, with a shallow end and a deep end. A diving board is this springy thing you jump off of to fall into the water. When you dive off the high board, you splash into the deep end of the pool and go far down."

"I get it," Gloria said, smiling. "I've never seen a swimming pool except in a movie, once – and I sure don't want to see one, that sounds scary – but you're saying I suddenly started talking about emotional stuff. Okay, what do I do? Take a couple of practice swings before we get to the deep stuff?"

"No, no."

"Helene," Susanna said, "Tom takes you as seriously as he can. But you had a fling with a guy the night before you met him, and now you're having an affair with him, and then you're going home and you'll find another guy. There's nothing wrong with that. Tom understands that you're giving him as much as you've got to give."

"It's wrong as all hell!" Helene said. "It's wrong even if I'm the one who's doing it. Honest to God, I don't understand you people. You spend all this effort and energy to cook delicious food when you're hungry, but when you want loving, you just go into town and open up a can of boyfriend."

"A can of boyfriend!" Gloria said, and they all laughed. "I like that! I'll remember that."

"Okay, okay," Helene said. "But still. Tom brought me into air town, we were lovers, now I've put myself back into my can and he thinks that ... I don't know, he thinks I can do that. I think *he* can do that. But that's not who I am, or anyway, it's not what I want."

Gloria said, "You want him to be jealous of this other guy you banged? Or do you want him to feel hurt because you had sex with another man? Or do you want *yourself* to be more hurt about having to go home than you actually are?"

"Maybe all of those. I can't think."

Susanna said suddenly, "Gregor and Yeni came back this morning. They're at work at the field now. They looked wonderful – radiant, really. You and

Tom were good friends to them when they needed it and you patched them up real good."

Helene looked at her. "Showing love to friends," Susanna continued, "that's love. That counts. What I'm trying to say is that you don't need to ask whether you are capable of love, or whether Tom is, because you *are*. You demonstrated that."

"Oh, I always knew I was capable," Helene said. "I was in love with a guy before, it didn't work out. It's too early to say I'm in love with Tom and I'm not in the most stable shape anyway because I *am* on a business trip and I *did* have a one-nighter with another guy and I want Tom to take me seriously at the exact same time I'm running away from him and I feel like this suit cuts me off from humanity and ..."

"Helene! Take a breath!" Gloria said.

"... and I need to stop and breathe," Helene said. "I don't know what I want. No, wait, I do. I want Tom. But I also know I can't have him."

"Okay, now we're getting somewhere," Susanna said. "Now, you know Tom's a straight-arrow even for a Moon Man, and as a group we're kind of famous for having sticks up our butts."

"You all and I actually do have a tube up our butts."

"Helene, congratulations!" Gloria said, smiling. "You have found a topic of conversation which is considered in bad taste to mention even for Moon Men. Not many people over the age of three have managed that."

"Wow, I didn't think that was possible."

"Anyway," Susanna said, "what I'm getting at is that you won't be able to hold on to Tom without marrying him. Some men are different, but I'm pretty sure that's what Tom will say. So that kind of puts the fish on the grill, doesn't it? Do you want him bad enough to marry him, or not?"

"I just met him four days ago!" Helene said.

"Understood."

"I just barely know him. I've never seen him in clothes that I didn't pick out for him. Maybe he's a mean drunk. If he wants kids that's a problem, and if he doesn't want kids that's a different problem. Maybe he watches porno inside his helmet when it's opaqued."

"He does," Gloria said after a moment, studying the display in her helmet, "but not very much, not as much as most guys, in fact, and nothing really icky. Well within normal parameters."

"And he has no more concept of privacy than you do. Gloria, Susanna, *I was not raised here.* I can't make that jump. I need to have personal space. I don't know if you can understand that, but it's really as important as oxygen, at least for me. And you can't ask me to give up looking at clouds in the sky, and swimming, and driving with the window down and ... and ... my *whole planet*, for God's sake."

"We're not asking you to give up anything," Gloria said quietly. "You're negotiating with yourself."

"I don't want to live on the Moon!" Helene said, and began to cry.

Gloria put her hand on Helene's shoulder, and Susanna did the same on her other side. They said nothing while Helene cried herself out.

"You might be able to talk Tom into going back with you. He loves you, even if neither one of you will say it. I think he might go if you asked him," Susanna said.

"Give up *his* whole world?" Helene said, sobbing. "I could never ask him for that. I'd hate myself, and if he did go to Earth he would hate me after a while."

After a long while, Gloria said "You need to tell Tom what you told us. It's always better to talk these things out."

"I can't talk to him. I can't see him. I can't keep him and I can't give him up. I can't go and I can't stay."

"You don't have to do anything right away," Susanna said. "If you don't want to stay with our family I can find you somebody else here who will take you in. You could even go back to air town and we'll tell Tom not to go after you."

"Thank you," Helene said. She stood up. Her face was still wet. "Really, thank you both more than I can say. But I've got a signature move I always use in situations like this."

"What's that?"

"I'm going to run away."

She walked away toward the terminal building on the field, being careful to stay inside the street lines until she was out of the village.

14: At Last, Meatloaf and Mashed Potatoes

The monorail took Helene racing across the nearly featureless expanse of Mare Serenitatis, riding a rack with her suitcase strapped into the seat beside her. It was a journey of an hour and a half which did not give her serenity but did allow her to calm down somewhat. She had stopped at the hotel in Theophrastus just long to retrieve her new suitcase, arrange with the bank to spend her money without a Moon suit, and get a reservation for her plane back home. She had not had time to get her new clothes washed, but the suitcase was not pressurized. She hoped the vacuum would allow Tom's scent to evaporate off before she had to wear her clothes again.

She looked up at the Night sky, her rack swinging slightly each time she moved her head, tracing the path of the Milky Way. There was no sky like it on Earth and certainly not in Chicago or any city a traveling salesman might be sent to. She drank it all in. She looked at Earth, too, and watched a storm work its way across Africa.

Presently the monorail rose up to cross the Lunar Appenines mountain range, much less spectacular at close view than they seemed from afar. They looked like rounded hills, covered with little speckles and craters, uninteresting. On the far side was the Appenines Mass Driver that would fling her plane back home, and the city of Eratosthenes Crater where she would board the plane.

On a sudden thought, she directed the rack away from the airlock at Eratosthenes, to the Moon

Man village outside the city. She walked from the monorail terminal into the village, which was just as empty and flat as Sinus Amoris village, and approached the first person she saw, whom her suit identified as Govinda Sativendra. His Moon suit was decorated with a picture of some large bridge on Earth, and there was an abstract design in the oval over his heart.

"Excuse me," she said without preliminaries, "can you tell me how I can ship my suit back to the Easterday Family in Sinus Amoris? I'm going to Earth and I won't need it. They paid for it."

"Hello, Helene," the man said, and studied the display in his helmet. "I'm sorry you're breaking up with, what's his name, Tom? But I'll tell you what, my wife's brother works for a company that ships machine parts all over, so if we can get your suit to them, I'll ask him to have it shipped back for you. You can pay his company for it. Hold on a moment." Govinda spoke for a minute without including Helene in the conversation. "Okay," he continued, "he says they can do it. You know, I can't ever remember seeing a whole suit in transit. That's going to be a little strange."

"Thank you. You can really do that? It's nice of you to take the trouble," Helene said.

"No problem. You're a Moon Man until you take off the suit, or in any event I'm going to play it that way, so I'm glad to help."

"I don't suppose too many Moon Men ever give up their suits, do they?"

"Sometimes kids going out for college or something," Govinda said. "But usually the family arranges to sell it back to the outfitter." He touched his finger to her interface port and an address in Eratosthenes appeared in her helmet. "Okay, when you get the suit off in air town, have them send it to that address and we'll get it back to the Easterdays for you. It'll probably cost about twelve sequins, so don't convert all your money to Earth money until that bill goes through. Helene, are you sure you want to do this? You're obviously pretty conflicted about it. You can stay here in our village for a while if that would help."

"I'm going back where people can't see my 38 instrument readings," Helene said grimly. "I can't tell you how I'm looking forward to that."

"All right, I won't pry. I went to Earth once and liked it. I'm sure you'll be happy there."

"Why did you go to Earth?"

"College. I'm a metallurgist, and I needed more education than I could get here. Also I just wanted to. I did a lot of tourist stuff while I was there, backpacked through Europe and things like that."

"Why did you come back?"

"This is where my life is."

Helene looked at him silently, then said, "Okay, thanks again, Govinda."

She retrieved her monorail rack and rode back up to the Moon Man airlock high on the crater wall. Eratosthenes crater was much larger than Theophrastus but the city portion was about the same size. Most of the rest of the area was agriculture and manufacturing that was more convenient to do in air than outside. The town served a port in Mare Ibrium as well as the mass driver that was used to toss cargo down to Earth. A car carried Helene past the usual casinos and tourist businesses to Earth Launch station.

Since the trip home took three days and she had only two changes of clothes, Helene took the opportunity to buy another outfit, which was fabricated while she was having her suit removed. The technician at the station was male, which Helene found slightly uncomfortable, but he was clearly working a bored routine as he extracted her from her suit.

She dressed herself in the clothes she had first picked out with Tom. Vacuum had boiled off all of the volatile oils the fabric had collected from her skin and his. Her clothes smelled, not washed, but lifeless. The technician, at her request, had put her suit back together for shipment. It slumped over without a person in it. Another terminal employee came to pick it up and have it delivered to the address Govinda had given her. She watched it being carried away, waited a few minutes to get her new clothes delivered by a robot cart, then walked out into the lobby of the terminal building.

Her old personal electronics had been built on Earth and had been destroyed by cold and vacuum along with her first suitcase. She purchased another device at a booth in the terminal building, a wide wristband which provided phone service, display and network connection, and strapped it on her wrist.

As soon as she closed the clasp, the phone rang.

The display lit up with Tom's face, from a camera inside his helmet. "Helene," he said, "stay right there. I'll be there in an hour. Don't go, please. We can figure this out."

"Tom, don't do this!" Helene said. "I'm sorry if I led you on. I'm so sorry. But I really was just having a fling while I'm far away from home. I didn't mean to hurt you, but Tom, we're not a couple. We never were, never will be."

"Not buying it. I know better than that, and you know I know it."

"Damn it, stop trying to analyze my data points and *listen* to me, you fool! We had one night together. That's all the relationship we ever had. It wasn't much and whatever little it was, it's over now."

"It is not over, and you're out of your suit so I couldn't read your data even if I hadn't promised not to. But I can see your face. Helene, I'm over Mare Serenitatis now. Just let me get there so I can see your face in ... you know, in air. I swear that's all I want right now."

"I won't be here. My plane leaves in a few minutes, and I'm going to be on it. Forget me, I'm going back home. Look, we never had more than two choices – you could go to Earth, or I could stay here. Either one's the booby prize. This never could have worked, I never meant it to, you never meant that much to me and I don't want see you!" She terminated the call.

She walked to the boarding area, showed her eyes to the scanner and went through an open airlock door to the shuttleplane bay.

Planes from Earth were thrown into lunar orbit by a tube up the side of Mt. Cotopaxi in Peru. From orbit, they were landed by Moon Men harbor pilots at various fields including Sinus Amoris and the field served from Eratosthenes. Planes going back were launched from the ground by the Lunar Appenines driver and were piloted directly to a landing at a field outside of Quito, to be returned to Cotopaxi for the next trip. Although cargo planes were launched and landed several times a day, there was only enough passenger traffic to support two planes, which held six passengers in a too-small compartment at the nose, along with a cargo hold that carried enough merchandise to make the trip profitable.

The plane Helene boarded happened to be the same one she had arrived in. The plane, a "lifting body" in which the wings were integral with the body, had been brought into the terminal air space. A rolling stair let her climb up to the door and enter the windowless cabin. There were four other passengers, who greeted her but were occupied in setting up their own spaces.

The pilot was the only crew member, but a steward came in to check that each person had stowed his possessions correctly. Helene strapped herself into the seat, by chance the same seat she had occupied on the flight up, and waited.

She was the last passenger. The steward left, the airlock was sealed and the plane was pulled out into vacuum. Helene watched through the window as the cargo bay was loaded by robots supervised by two Moon Men. It seemed strange to her to see their bulky, smooth forms but not know their names or family relationships. The cargo was tanks of helium-3, which was cooked out of the Moon dust and was valuable to power plants on Earth. When all the tanks had been stowed, the plane was dragged to the opening of the mass driver tube.

Launching from the Moon was much simpler than launching from Earth. The mass driver required vacuum all along the path, from the horizontal start to the near-vertical end. On Earth, that meant an elaborate (and to Helene, scary) series of snap-open doors that would slide back just long enough to allow the magnets to drive the shuttleplane forward, then close in an instant so that any air that entered could be pumped out for the next shot. But the mass driver on the Moon was just a series of open rings going up the mountain side.

The plane was wheeled into position at the first ring. Without any further preliminaries, Helene was pressed back into her seat as the plane was grabbed by magnetic fields and smoothly accelerated up through the rings. It reached a gentle maximum of two gravities as it burst out of the mass driver at the top of the mountain, and went immediately weightless. Her stomach lurched.

After that, the passengers faced three days of boredom before reaching Earth.

Weightlessness had been only slightly interesting on the trip out, once Helene had gotten anti-nausea drugs. The cabin did not have the space to fly around without passing close enough to the other seats to annoy the occupants. On the way up, she had done a few tricks such as parking objects in front of her face to marvel that they hung in the air and did not fall, but even that meager fun was not interesting a second time.

Tom called after a few minutes. "I'm just coming into Eratosthenes," he said breathlessly. "I'll be there in a couple of minutes."

"I'm already in space," Helene said, looking at him steadily. "You're too late. Tom, go home. You're making a big deal about this but we were never that close, really."

"You don't mean that. I know you don't."

"I'm going home, Tom. You too." She ended the call.

The seats across from her were occupied by an elderly couple. The woman leaned forward and said, "What I always like about travel is the chance to meet other people, especially on a flight like this where we'll have enough time for some really good conversation. I'm Carolina Madison and this is my husband Alex."

"Um, hi. I'm Helene Friedman."

"Are you from Earth?"

"Yes, I am."

"How wonderful! We're going to Earth for a historical tour, it's something we've always wanted to do and now that we're retired, we finally have the time. We're going to Greece and Rome and the old medieval cities in Europe and everything. It must be marvelous to actually live on Earth and be able to see all that history. We're from Second Amendment."

"Second Amendment? That's the name of your planet?" Helene asked.

"Yes, it's historical. We've always been interested in history. Our planet doesn't have very much history since it was only settled about ninety years ago, but of course Earth is so ancient and cultured and civilized. You must think we're country bumpkins compared to the people you know on Earth."

"No, no. We're just regular people on Earth."

"Oh, everyone says that about their own culture, don't you think? That's why it's so fascinating to travel. We've been to two other worlds, ourselves. Here, I've got some pictures."

Helene said desperately, "On my schedule it's bedtime, so I'll have to beg off. Nice talking to you." She pulled up the privacy curtains around her seat, and was in a space with featureless white fabric walls, two meters across and three high.

It was not actually bed time for her yet. She tapped on her wristband device to find a book she had not read, then pulled a tray of warm food out of a slot in the base of her chair. The food was especially portioned and packaged to be eaten in zero gravity. It was meatloaf and mashed potatoes, but her ticket included unlimited refills on wine.

15: The Orchestra is Out to Lunch

Helene's Moon suit arrived at the Easterday compound about the same time Tom came back. It was bedtime for them by then; Tom said nothing to anyone and they respected his silence. He picked the suit up disconsolately and carried it over to the sleeping area. The air pressure inside stiffened the arms and legs, pointing them straight away from the trunk. When he tried to put the suit in a sitting position on the ground, the weight of the backpack pulled it down. Her suit lay facing upward, arms and legs splayed out foolishly, the helmet empty.

He plugged himself into a post and sat next to her suit to sleep.

*　　*　　*

On the second day, Tom called, but Helene refused to answer. She kept her curtain-wall up, drank wine, read books and watched movies. Every couple of hours she emerged to use the head, nodded to the Madisons, then hid herself again.

Apparently, by dating Tom Easterday, Helene seemed to have started a relationship with half of the population of Sinus Amoris village. The phone rang a little later from a caller Helene did not recognize, and she cautiously answered it. A blonde woman appeared. "Hi, Helene?" she said. "I'm Lindsay Amundsen, you don't know me, but my family is a customer of Tom's shop. He just has the best, freshest spices and I know he buys a lot of them from you."

"Yes, he does," Helene said, bewildered. The conversation was made even a little stranger by the slight but noticeable speed-of-light delay added to each exchange, as the shuttleplane neared the halfway point between Earth and Moon.

"Well, I just wanted to say that I hope you'll get back together with him. He's awfully sad about losing you and I wanted you to know how much you mean to him."

"You're one of Tom's *customers* and you're calling me about my love life?" Helene said, a little slurred. "Are you people fresh out of your ethnic village minds or what? Who does that?"

"We look out for each other around here," Lindsay said. "I know you're from Earth, and I know what Earth people are like. But I don't think Tom understood that."

"What are Earth people like?" Helene said.

"You're all uneasy because you have to breathe each other's air and smell each other's sweat and farts, so you get all withdrawn and don't communicate and don't open yourselves up for love or any kind of relationships."

"You got us," Helene said. "That's exactly who we are. Not only that, we're rude to strangers who call to tell us bullshit." She terminated the call.

Gloria Beacon called. Helene answered and said, "Hello, Gloria. Don't say one damn word about Tom." She sipped at her wine, holding the pouch up where Gloria could see it.

Gloria blinked, then said, "Okay. Okay. Um, how's your trip going?"

"I'm floating around like a party balloon inside my little curtained cubicle. I only go out to use the head and then I have to look real angry so nobody tries to talk to me. How are you?"

"I'm fine. How's the wine?"

"Just wonderful. Moon wine has terrific *terroir*, which is that special flavor it gets from the soil. Or in this case, the flavor of grapes that are grown on wires under electric lights and have their roots piddled on by robots." Helene took another pull at the pouch.

"Settle down, Helene. Can I tell you about your Moon suit?" Gloria asked.

"What about it? I sent it back. Didn't Tom or somebody get it?"

"Oh, he got it, all right. It's lying on the ground with the arms and legs sticking out, right next to his sleeping space. He says he's going to keep it because he thinks you'll come back. Girl, do you have any idea how odd it is for a Moon Man to own something that isn't useful? I know on Earth, people have houses that are all cluttered up with stuff, but right now Tom is the only guy in Sinus Amoris who owns a big useless object like that."

"I thought you were going to sell it back to that woman in air town or something. I mean, I know it can be broken up into parts that all get re-used, right?"

"Only after your ex-boyfriend decides to let it go. Which he is not showing any signs of doing."

"Crap. Gloria, will you tell him I'm not coming back? Tom is crazy but you know I have to go home, right?"

"Hell, no. Since the suit's still activated, I can see your readings up until the time you took it off. You might still wind up coming back, the way you feel. I'm with Tom on this one."

"I'm an Earth woman," Helene said. "I need to go smell other Earth people's sweat and farts." She terminated the call.

Lunch was a hamburger wrapped in paper to keep the pieces together, along with re-heated french fries. In the afternoon, Tom's parents called. "Oh, God," Helene said ungraciously. "Hello, uh, Mr. and Mrs. Easterday. Who's next after you, the Ghost of Christmas Past?"

"Harper and Louisa, dear," his mother said. "I don't understand the other thing."

"Don't worry about it, I'm just drunk," Helene said helplessly. "You're calling to tell me I should go back to Tom?"

"Of course we are," Louisa said.

"You're the kind of ethnics who have arranged marriages, aren't you? The parents set their kids up to be married and you've decided I'm supposed to marry Tom. It doesn't work that way in *my* village!"

"Of course we have arranged marriages," Harper said. "Did you know our divorce rate is among the lowest of any nation on any planet? But not arranged by the parents. Our marriages are arranged by the data. When you love somebody, it shows up in your skin conductance, in your blood chemistry, the pupils of your eyes when you look at your beloved – lots of things. We know you love Tom, and he loves you. Nobody else here is anything like as good of a match."

"Then it's too bad I'm a couple of hundred thousand kilometers away," Helene said. "Goodbye."

*   *   *

Tom and Gregor stood next to one of the Easterday food carts. "It's not just weightlessness," Gregor said, "although that's bad enough. Have you ever been in free-fall?"

"Just a couple of school trips," Tom said. It was Monday and Tom had drawn kitchen duty, which was always something of an event for the Easterday family since he was an especially good cook. Gregor was able to match up his schedule enough to come visit at supper time. All around them, the Easterday family

169

sat and stood, chatting with each other. Tom and Gregor spoke privately.

"Then if you go to Earth, make sure they get you some good nausea drugs," Gregor said. "A quick school trip and three days floating around are two different things. Anyway, what I'm getting at is that right about now, Helene's shuttle will be entering atmosphere. It's a skip-glide approach – they go into the atmosphere to slow down, which means some acceleration, then they come up out of the atmosphere where they're weightless again to cool off, then back down. They go all the way around about twice before they slow down enough to stay in the air and land. Weight and float, weight and float, weight and float – if Helene hasn't tossed her cookies before, she's doing it now."

"Thank you for sharing that before dinner," Tom said sourly. He was mincing fresh ginger for chicken teriyaki meatballs, part of a dinner called *The Savor of a Bitter-Sweet Memory*.

"Two points," Gregor persisted. "One, if you ever talk to Helene about coming back here, she's going to remember this trip and think 'Hell, no, I'm not going through that again.' Two, if you go to her then *you* have to ride the vomit-comet down to the ground. All I'm saying is the same thing Helene said to you – every choice is the booby prize."

"And thanks even more for sharing that." Tom raised his voice, causing the network to distribute his voice generally to the people nearby. "Supper will be ready in a few minutes," he said. "My old friend Gregor has just given me some excellent advice, which is 'Boy, are you screwed.' Anybody *else* have any words of wisdom for me? Come one, come all."

"Tom, it's not going to make a blind bit of difference what we say when you're dithering like you are right now," his mother said reasonably. "You're sweating and you're not working that hard. Look, you can't do anything about Helene or anything else until after you finish cooking. So give yourself a break for that long, at least."

The other people cooking that day were Tom's cousin Maris and his father. Maris said "The veggie balls are done. I'm keeping them warm but I can't hold them too much longer before they start getting hard."

"These don't take long," Tom muttered. He mashed the ginger and other ingredients into ground chicken, formed the goop into balls and popped them into boiling water. As they came ready, he passed the cooked meatballs in a transfer container to his father, who efficiently doused them with teriyaki sauce, then loaded them into sixpacks along with the veggie balls and rolls from Maris, and dessert he had made himself.

"Suppertime!" his father said, and everyone lined up to get food. When everyone had been served, Tom sat down with Gregor and his immediate family.

"Tom, even if I didn't have any other information, I can tell you're upset because these meatballs aren't as good as you usually make them," his mother said.

Because he was judging food, Tom instantly switched gears and became thoughtful and objective. He ate one of the meatballs and said, "You're right. I *am* worked up, these weren't boiled for the right length of time. It's been three days now and I'm not handling this any better than I did at first."

"I've been trying to avoid mentioning that empty zombie suit laying on its back over there," his father said, "but it's starting to be a little creepy. Shouldn't we get that back into air-town and get some money for it? You could give the money to Gregor and Yeni, it came from their wedding party and it would be a nice wedding gift for them."

"We don't need that," Gregor said quickly. "We're doing okay. I don't think Tom is ready to let go of that suit yet, anyway. I mean, it's kind of pathetic but we can pretend for a while that maybe she's coming back."

"It doesn't cost that much to make the trip," Tom said stoutly. "If we got married, I could go to Earth to visit or she could come here to visit. Once in a while, anyway. This could still work out."

"Tom, did you loan that girl some neurons she forgot to give back?" Gregor said. "You are being stark, staring stark and staring."

"I finally got the proceeds from that rockfall I invested in," Tom said out of nowhere. "I made some pretty good money on that."

"So there you are," his mother said. "You're young, good-looking, you can cook when you have your mind on it and you're semi-rich. If you get out of the family compound, you can easily meet a nice girl you're not related to."

"I've got enough for a ticket to Earth," Tom said.

"Well, let's explore that," Gregor said. "If you get a one-way ticket to Earth, you go there and maybe Helene takes you back and maybe she doesn't. If not, you have to buy a ticket back and you've wasted a bunch of money, not to mention being emotionally crippled for the rest of your life, plus you've spent a lot of time throwing up. If she says yes, you have to live on Earth, away from your family and friends and work, isolated and lonely because you will never know anything about another human being except what you see and hear through the air. Pretty soon you're depressed."

"Or," Gregor continued, "maybe you convince Helene to come back here. You spend even more money for tickets for both of you. Helene has to live here, convinced that she has made a bad bargain — she lives her whole life in a can, in exchange for getting a husband. Pretty soon she decides the husband she got may be okay but he's not worth *that* much, and she's depressed."

"Anybody got any *useful* advice?" Tom asked.

"You have to do what your heart tells you to do," his mother said.

"That sounds like a song cue," Tom said. He looked around. "But apparently the orchestra is out to lunch or something."

"You've got three choices," Gregor said. "You can go, or you can stay. You can't do the third choice here because we don't *have* any walls, but you could also go into air town and bang your head against a wall there until you pass out, or come to your senses, whichever comes first."

"At last, some useful advice," Tom said, standing. "Mom, Dad, Gregor, I need you to do me some favors. Tell the kids who work for me to fill any orders we have, then shut the business down until I get back. I love you all, I'm out of here."

He walked away, toward the passenger terminal, being careful to stay inside the street lines.

*   *   *

Helene lurched unsteadily out of the shuttleplane, dropping two warm, full sick bags into the container the company had thoughtfully provided at the door. She took one step at a time down the rolling stair, clutching the handrails, then got into the little cart (driven by a human driver, she was somewhat bemused to see) and was taken to the terminal building at Quito Field. She looked up into the blue sky and thought she should smile, but didn't.

She slept through the flight from Quito to Mexico City. In an airport restaurant, she ordered enchiladas, which she cut into bite-sized pieces and ate carefully, alternating with bites of beans, rice and avocado. She slept again from Mexico City to Chicago, took a cab back to her apartment, and fell into her bed with her clothes on.

*   *   *

Tom sent his empty suit back from air town, rather than pay rental on a storage locker. His parents laid it on its back, on the ground next to Helene's suit. Because both suits were stiff with internal air pressure, both faced upward, not looking at each other. Tom's mother regarded them for a moment, then nudged Tom's suit so the out-flung left hand touched the right hand of Helene's suit.

16: The List of Pressure Points

It was late on an overcast day in Quito when Tom walked down the stair from the shuttleplane and first touched the ground of Earth. He had not quite been sick, but when he looked up into the gray sky the movement of his head made him stumble a little. He was amazed to see that the airport cart was driven by a man in a uniform. Was he a peasant who had been given a make-work job? A convict? Some kind of hereditary thing? He climbed into the cart with the other passengers and gave the driver a stiff, awkward nod.

The lumpy clouds in the sky moved as he looked at them, which reinforced his queasiness.

He spent the flight to Mexico City in an aisle seat, trying to read magazines. At an airport restaurant, he ordered enchiladas and managed to get mole sauce all over his face and part of the shirt he had bought with Helene. He was nervous and awake, watching news broadcasts with little comprehension, on the flight to Chicago. The sight of stewards walking up and down the aisles, not secured by harnesses and without armor against collisions, raised more questions than he could cope with: he wound up saying nothing to them and did not get any drinks.

He called Helene when his plane was approaching the airport. She answered in her nightgown, sleepy and blinking. "Tom? What the hell? Where are you?"

"I'm on the plane coming into Ohare Airport," he said. "Can you come meet me?"

"You're *here*? Tom, I ran away from you. We're not together. What the hell are you doing?"

"So I just ran toward you. We can be together when you meet me at the airport."

"Do you have any idea what time it is? It's two in the morning here!"

"What part of your day is that? I can't keep track after three days in transit."

"It's the middle of the damn night, that's what!"

"Helene, please come meet me."

She looked out at him from his wristband. "Did you throw up," she asked, "on the atmosphere approach?"

"Almost, but I kept it down," Tom said.

"You must have wanted to come here pretty bad."

"You have no idea. Or wait, I hope maybe you do have an idea."

"All right. I'll be at the airport in half an hour. I'll call you when I get there."

Tom had never seen anyone or anything flying that was shaped like an airplane. He spent his last half-hour in the air searching for articles on "How Do Airplanes Fly?", was completely dissatisfied with the explanations he found, and had worked himself into a minor panic by the time the plane touched down. He left the airplane by a covered walkway and did not see the night sky.

The airport terminal, however, seemed familiar and homely when he entered it, a hundred times the size of the terminal at Sinus Amoris but populated by much the same kind of travelers. He even saw a few passengers in Hawaiian shirts. Helene called, and with her help and many wrong detours, he managed to get out to the terminal lobby to meet her.

The season was early autumn in Chicago. Helene wore a light brown leather coat belted at the waist, and even that vague suggestion of her figure made his heart leap when he looked at her. She had her hair pulled back with a band, she was bleary-eyed from sleep, she was carrying a brown sweater under her arm, and she looked beautiful.

He held out his arms when he saw her. She frowned, hesitated, then opened her arms and embraced him when they met. She did not kiss him. When she stepped back, she handed him the sweater. "I figured you'd show up with just that shirt," she said. "It's cold in the mornings this time of year. Put this on."

He pulled on the sweater, saying "Helene, I ..."

"Tom, there are fifty couples in this hall doing big reunion scenes," Helene said. "Let's save it for a while. Come on, I'll take you out for breakfast. My car's in the lot."

They walked through the cavernous parking garage. "You own a car all for yourself?" Tom asked.

"Yeah. As a salesman, I have to go to a lot of weird locations and sometimes I can't pick up a driverless, so I have a car and I can drive it myself. A lot of people don't, but I have a license to operate a car manually," she said. When they reached her car, Tom balked at entering in it without quite knowing why. It took him a moment to realize that the windows bothered him because they were too thin to hold air pressure, and then to reassure himself that they did not have to. Helene waited for him with some asperity.

When they exited the garage, Tom was introduced to the concept of paying for parking, something he had never deduced from watching movies set on Earth.

In the early-morning darkness, the traffic was light. Tom stared out the window at the stores and houses they passed. "Everything seems ... I don't know, old, kind of worn down," he remarked tactlessly. "Is it just this area?"

"It's everywhere, as far as I've seen, and I've seen more than most people," Helene said. "For a hundred years, anybody with any get-up-and-go has emigrated to one of the planets. We're the ones who were left, we don't have as much energy as people used to, and a lot of things like houses are starting to wear out now. Welcome to Earth."

The twenty-four-hour restaurant was quiet when they entered, except for banal background music. It was close enough to the expressway to attract a fair number of patrons, but the pre-dawn atmosphere left them all silent and withdrawn. A waitress led them to a booth, past diners sitting solitary, in couples and in groups, but all hunched over their food, reading the news or other text on various devices. Tom looked hard at men who appeared to be construction workers getting ready for the day's work, who sat together without speaking. They passed a man and woman dressed in social clothes, apparently at the end of a date, who also sat without speaking. No one looked back at him.

When they were seated, they ordered breakfast. Out of her coat, Helene wore a soft blue woolen dress. "Are you okay now, Tom?" she asked, speaking in a voice low enough that the people in the next booth would not be able to hear her. "You were puffing just from the walk to the car. I think full gravity's harder on you than you thought it would be."

"I'm okay," Tom said. He instinctively kept his voice low as well. "I feel a little heavier, but also, every time I move my arms and legs it feels like they're shooting forward because I'm not getting any resistance from my suit. But I'll get used to this."

He was silent for a while, looking at her. Helene said, even more quietly, "Don't stare at my chest like that. That's rude. Hello? Earth to Tom?" Then she glanced down at herself, and said, "Oh. Tom, this is where they're actually supposed to be. I guess there are some things I liked about one-sixth gravity."

"Do you know, people who live on the Moon live about twenty years longer than people on planets? One-sixth gravity really eases the strain on your heart."

"Do you know, you should go back there then and live twenty years longer? Tom, you don't belong here and I don't belong there. If you were to stay here, you'd live twenty years *less*."

"But I'd be with you."

"No, you'd be living with some other woman because there's no way in hell I'm going to let a man die twenty years early for me. But for God's sake, Tom, do you realize this is pretty much our *second date*? You can't be talking about a lifetime already."

"No, wait," Tom said. "We played pitch and toss together, which was sort of a date, then we watched the rockfall, that counts as a date. Then we went to air town, and the next day we went to the vineyard and then we went flying, that's three dates right there."

Helene just looked at him, then shook her head. Tom said, "It's been enough time for me to say I love you. I do love you."

The waitress arrived with their food and Helene was spared from having to reply. Tom closed his eyes a moment and said a brief silent grace over his food.

"That saying-grace thing, is that something that's important to you?" Helene asked, when the waitress had left.

"It's kind of important. You don't have to do it."

"You're a member of the First Baptist Flat Piece of Ground back home, and I'm an agnostic Jew. We'll just add that to the list of pressure points," Helene said. After a moment, she added, "You know, for a gourmet who loves food as much as you do, you hold your fork like a little kid."

"I haven't had much practice with forks," Tom muttered.

"Here," Helene said gently, and touched his hand. "Not with your fist. Open your hand, then hold it like this. Good, that's better."

"As a boyfriend," Tom said, "I'm not providing much leadership in this relationship, am I?"

"You're not my boyfriend. You're very dear to me, but this can't work and we both know it. You need to go home to the Moon, and go check out every unmarried Moon Man woman one at a time until you meet the one who gives you the right 38 data points.

Sooner or later you will meet a nice girl who gives you high skin conductivity or low skin conductivity, whichever one you're supposed to have, and then you'll know it's true love."

"Helene, I came one and a quarter light-seconds here to tell you I love you."

"And I drove to and from the airport to tell you, 'No.'"

"No, you don't love me, or no, you won't let me love you?"

"Let's just leave it at 'No'," Helene said. "And, Tom, please, don't make me say that again. I hate saying that to you."

"I'm not crazy about it either." They ate in silence for a while, and finally Tom said, "They always say everybody talks about the weather, so hey, how about that weather outside, huh?"

"It's supposed to be a pretty nice day today," Helene said. "But Tom, do you see how far out of position you are? At home you sit around with your family in minus 150 degrees and it doesn't seem odd to you, but when you got here I had to tell you that it gets cold at three in the morning. Tom, we're just too different."

"I wasn't asking for another reason why this relationship is doomed," Tom said.

"No, you weren't. I'm sorry. It's all I can think about, looking at you."

"Maybe it's not romantic, but I look at you and I think about seeing you in that hotel room. That was a pretty wonderful night, wasn't it?"

She smiled shyly. "Yes, it was. Also the next morning. Tom, I wish we'd had more time together."

"We're together now."

She just shook her head again, slowly. "I can't believe in it, anymore. Your Mom and Dad called me again. They told me you left your suit with them. Tom, you still want to go back, you know you do. You wouldn't have left your suit if you didn't expect to go back to it."

Tom looked at her. "Why did you send your suit to me, instead of just cashing it in?"

Helene drank more coffee. "It's so nice to drink coffee out of a cup," she remarked irrelevantly. "Rather than sucking it through a straw. I guess ... I don't know, when you've been that intimate with an object, it's kind of hard to let it go to strangers, you know?"

"I do know. You've got some Moon Man in you now, haven't you? We rubbed off on you."

"Yeah. That's not a good thing."

Tom stood up. "I have to go to the washroom," he said. "That's another thing about Moon Men, we never really learn much bladder control, since we don't need to."

Helene hissed, "Also, you never learn to not make remarks like a toddler when you're in a public restaurant! Just go! Don't tell me about it!"

"Oh, hush! You worry so much about what you can say and what you can't say that you and all the other mouth-breathers never say anything that means anything."

"Tom, do you know you're a damn bigot?" All around them, heads turned at the sound of Helene's voice. "You're calling *us* names? You M-M's have the social skills of oysters! You never come out of your shells and you think that makes you superior to natural human beings?"

"Social skills!" Tom yelled. "What in hell would you or any other Earthman know about social skills? Look at 'em all here!" He waved his hands at the faces now turning toward them from all directions. "You're all isolated, sitting with your heads down, lonely as hell. On the Moon, we'd be talking with each other, gossiping, chatting, being social. I walked in here, I'm a stranger in town, and nobody as much as said hello. A Moon Man can go to any village in any port and everybody will call you by name, ask how you are, talk to you like they value you as a person. You people can't even talk to people you know."

Helene stood as well. "Then why don't you go back to your village? Your little ethnic community where everybody's your buddy and everybody can see your blood-sugar level and everybody knows everything you eat and every time you take a dump! You've got no right to come down here and tell me I'm lonely. I'm not lonely, I'm normal! All of these people, they're all normal! You're the one who's weird and that is *not* a compliment! Why are you here?"

"Because I love you."

"I love you too, you jerk, but I also know how to go to the bathroom without having to announce it to the world!"

"You love me too?" Tom asked.

"Yeah, I figured that out, like, day before yesterday. But it still doesn't change anything." Helene pulled a bill out of her purse and laid it on the table, then said, "Let's get out of here."

"Kiss him!" somebody laughed, and three or four people started tapping on their glasses with spoons.

Tom turned to the nearest one and asked, "What does that mean?"

"It means you should kiss her, you jerk." There was more laughter all around.

Tom looked around at all the eyes watching him, his own eyes wide and frightened. Helene said quietly, "Come on, Tom. Can you hold it for a little while longer?"

"Um, yeah."

"Then let's go."

Outside, the sun had risen and the air was fresh and cool with dawn. Tom walked through the door and stopped so abruptly that Helene almost walked into him. He was staring up into the cloudless blue sky. "Tom?" Helene asked.

He turned unsteadily, his eyes wild, then spun a second time. "Tom, what's wrong?" Helene asked.

"There's no ... you know, *thing* overhead," Tom stuttered helplessly. "Not anything. Roof, lid, dome, you know what I mean. Nothing holds the air in. It could out-gas in, in, in minutes." He drew a deep ragged breath and leaned back, craning his neck to see straight up.

Helene took his arm. "Tom, it's okay. Don't worry. It's always like this."

"Empty ... the air is just ... " Tom gasped. His eyes rolled up, and he fainted and fell.

17: Gravity is Good for Something

"We've got your tests back," the doctor said to Tom, "and you don't have any of the medical markers for agoraphobia."

"So I just freaked out?" Tom said. Helene was sitting at the side of his hospital bed, holding his hand. As a precaution against another freak-out, all of the windows in the room were covered with curtains to shut out any glimpse of the sunny day outside.

"Laymen should not try to use technical terminology," the doctor said. She smiled, and was pretty enough to give Helene a little twinge of jealousy. "Otherwise, why would you have to pay us? Okay, so here's what you need to know. You have what's called 'cognitive agoraphobia,' which means you talked yourself into this condition and you can talk yourself out of it again – it's not a pathology that needs to be treated with medicine. I looked it up, and apparently this happens to other Moon Men pretty regularly. It's just that we don't see you on Earth all that often. Anyway, you actually do know that gravity holds down the air and has for a zillion years. You just have convince yourself of that before you walk out under the open sky again. In the meantime, try to always keep a roof over your head while you're here. If you have to go outside, get a hat with a brim you can pull down. You can leave the hospital now, and you should be fine."

"How about the bump where he banged his head on the sidewalk?" Helene asked.

"We checked the scan, and there's no concussion," the doctor said. "We'll give you some pills for your headache, and that will go away too."

"Thank you," Tom said.

"Is it okay if I open the windows?" Helene asked, and the doctor nodded.

"Yeah, go ahead," Tom said. "I get it, I'm okay now. That blue sky just caught me when I had a lot on my mind about other things." The doctor left, and he got out of bed, walked with as much dignity as he could in a hospital gown to the locker, and retrieved his clothes. Helene opened the curtains to let in the sunlight.

They cleared up remaining details at the front desk, and then Helene led him to the gift shop. The only hats they had were white cowboy hats with "Chicago North Community Hospital" written on them. "You're kidding me," Tom said. "You want me to wear that?"

"Either you wear it or I don't let you outside of this building," Helene said. "You heard the doctor."

"It's for kids!"

"It says one size fits all."

Tom submitted. They bought the hat, and Tom pulled it down so tightly that the brim obscured his view of the sky. The tight band made his headache worse. They went outside to the parking lot and sought out Helene's car. "You're not stable yet," Helene said. "Hold on to my arm."

"I weigh too much, and my arms and legs don't work the way I'm used to," Tom said. "It's not agoraphobia or the bump on my head."

"You still hold on to me."

"Helene, thanks for taking care of me," Tom said. "I love you."

"I love you, too," Helene said, and sighed, "We are *so* screwed."

Tom was better inside the car, with a roof over his head again. The day was nice enough to roll down the windows, but Helene thoughtfully kept the windows up and the air conditioner on, to suggest a barrier against the outside air. He pulled off the cowboy hat with some difficulty. "Where should we go?" he asked.

"Back to my place, I guess," Helene said. "It doesn't make sense to put you in a hotel, and I don't know where else we should go."

"I should have asked before, do you need to go to work or something?"

"I don't have a job, remember? Actually, I'm going to ask for my old job back. Since I'm a salesman who gets pretty good orders, they'll probably take me. But I haven't done it yet, I needed a couple of days off. I am supposed to see my parents for supper. You might as well meet them."

They drove through quiet residential streets. In the daylight, the houses were even shabbier than by night, and Tom saw many that were abandoned. "This looks like the neighborhoods in movies," Tom said. "Movies that are fifty years old or more."

"Things don't change much on Earth anymore. All the changes are happening on the planets, because that's where all the people who make changes have gone."

"What kind of food do you have at home?" he asked suddenly.

"Nothing much. We were just going to go out to a restaurant."

"You have stores here with food you can buy, right? Why don't we get something and I'll cook it?"

"Oh, god. Don't tell me you don't have grocery stores on the Moon."

"I think they have them in air town, for the locals. Travelers eat in restaurants and Moon Men order food for the whole family from wholesalers. I've never actually been in a grocery store, no."

"You're just having one new experience after another, aren't you? Okay, there's a place up ahead. Come to think of it, wasn't that your big move with the ladies back home, to cook spiced meatballs for them?"

"You bet. It worked, pretty often. Think it'll work on you?"

Helene glanced at him while driving. "Listen, lover boy, you have *already* worked on me. Any more work on my emotions, is just twisting the knife."

Tom looked down, then said, "I'll make you and your folks some good food. I know a big twenty-bite meal called *A Fleeting Scent Recalls a Fading Memory*. Want to try that?"

"Why, that sounds delicious. My parents would love a hot wad of Fading Memory. Does it come with Fleeting Scent sauce?"

"It's lamb meatballs with ..."

"Don't tell me. Don't tell my Mom and Dad, either, they hate it when I take them to weird ethnic restaurants. You understand we're just going to slap all the food on big plates and eat it in any order, so the meal will be totally incoherent, right?"

188

"Right. That's okay, I'm feeling pretty incoherent myself," Tom said.

Tom had to put his cowboy hat back on before Helene would let him walk into the grocery store. He was astonished by the scents and smells of all the fresh produce and meats, amazed by all the food in cans. "Putting stuff in cans," he said, "doesn't that affect the flavor?"

"Of course it does. You don't have cans?"

"There's no sense paying the freight to lift steel cans from Earth, and nobody on the Moon packs food that way. We just get everything in plastic bags. But if I ever get back, I should special-order some cans of something. It would be an interesting change of taste, I bet."

"I wouldn't plan on that," Helene said.

"How many people am I cooking for?"

"Just four."

"Your parents aren't bringing anybody else? Don't you have other family members in the area?"

"My brother and sister, and their families. They're not coming tonight."

"Older, or younger?"

"Younger," Helene said. "I'm the oldest. Yeah, they both have families and I'm still single."

Tom looked at her. "Okay, then," he said. He had converted quite a bit of his money to currency he could spend on Earth, and wound up touring up and down all the aisles, filling his shopping cart with more food than Helene would ordinarily bring home in a month. When they got back to the parking lot, wearing the cowboy hat again, he was so winded from the experience that she had to load it all into her car herself.

"Home, sweet home," Helene announced, as she pulled into the parking lot of her building. It was a small apartment building of pale brick, with six units.

Tom looked it over from the car. "The building protects you against the weather?"

"Yeah, I guess you could say that's what it's for."

"Solid brick and glass and concrete like that, the weather must be pretty fierce. What do you have in Chicago? Hurricanes, snow storms, tornadoes?"

"No, yes, not usually, and because this is Chicago, in answer to any other question about the weather, yes. Help me carry this stuff inside, please."

"I don't want to wear this hat anymore."

"It's okay, I'm on the ground floor and we're parked right next to the door. Keep your eyes down, will you?"

Tom carried bags in, his eyes on the ground, and followed her into her apartment. He looked around at the kitchen while she put the food away. "All of this, set up all the time even when you're not at home or not cooking," he said. "I guess it makes sense, it just seems strange."

"Also a living room, set up even when I'm not living in it," Helene said. "Which is most of the time, when I'm working. Also a bed, which stays right there even when I'm not sleeping in it. We've got a few hours before my folks get here. Want to see the bedroom?"

Tom looked at her, his eyes bleak. "Is that a good idea?" he asked.

She came to him, embraced and kissed him. "It's going to hurt like hell when you have to go and I have to stay," she said. "You've hurt me pretty bad by following me to Earth, and I'm still kind of mad about it. But do you think it's going to hurt less if we don't spend the afternoon making love? We haven't got any way to make this better, but being together now isn't going to make it worse."

"That's the worst reason for sex I think I've ever heard."

"When we're in bed, I can get half on top of you and the gravity will pull my body down onto yours," she murmured. "Press us together. Me and you, skin touching skin."

"I knew this gravity was good for something," he said.

18: Sweet is the Night Air!

"We have a lot of weird restaurants in this city," Fred Friedman, Helene's father, said. "Little places that have fusions of two kinds of cuisines you never heard of. Last one I heard of was one of the colony planets, I think Prester John, plus French."

"Somebody from Prester John emigrated back to Earth to start a restaurant?" Tom said, raising his eyebrows.

"Fat chance. I don't actually know, but I think the place I'm thinking of was started by an Earthman who found a book of recipes from Prester John, but never actually went there," Fred said. "However, they didn't do so good. There's kind of a prejudice against off-planet stuff. Anyway, I was going to say, this is really good. I mean really good. If you're going to stay here, you could start a restaurant with authentic Moon Man cuisine and I bet it would make money. You'd just have to call it something else."

"People here don't like Moon Men either?"

"They don't like the planets because they're draining our economy," Fred said. "I don't think most people have ever heard of Moon Men – I don't think I ever did, until right now – but if it sounds off-planet, I bet they won't try the food. You understand, I'm not prejudiced. I get along with everybody. Besides, if you move here, you're automatically an Earth man."

"Dad, he can't stay here," Helene said. "People die early from living on Earth."

"People die early," her mother Deborah said dreamily, "from eating food like this. Tom, is this really the kind of sauce you people regularly put on vegetables? I mean, it's delightful, but how do you all avoid getting fat? I'm sure I've eaten half a pound of these and probably gained a full pound doing it. I don't even know how that's physically possible but I can feel it just the same."

"Well, it's not exactly the same sauce," Tom said. "We use a sticky sauce that holds everything together into balls, although it tastes about the same. I just couldn't find the ingredients here. But we have an advantage besides the lunar gravity – we get our blood-lipid readings taken continually. Even if you don't notice your own blood getting too much fat, somebody else is sure to mention it to you."

"He's right about that," Helene said. "You think you get fat-shamed for eating a hamburger? In Tom's village, total strangers will come up and tell you what was wrong with the lunch you ate an hour ago, before you even met them. I mean, that's like a *conversation starter* for them."

"From what Helene tells us about Moon Men," Fred said, "I kind of wonder what you do talk about? I mean, just in Chicago we have the Forest Preserves, we have city parks where people walk dogs, we have waves crashing on the beach from Lake Michigan, we look up at the Moon in the night sky. You don't have any of those things."

"Fredrick Friedman, you old stodge," Deborah said, "the last time you were in the Forest Preserve it was when your union had a beer party, and you never got out of the picnic grove. You only go to the park when the grandkids come over, which is maybe twice a year. This apartment is six blocks from Lake Michigan and we haven't been there once this summer, and the last time you noticed the Moon I told you, 'Look, honey, the Moon looks nice,' and you said, and I quote, 'Yeah.'"

"Come to think of it," Helene said, "the Moon's up now and we can see it from the window. Tom, do you want to try to look?"

"Why shouldn't he look?" Deborah asked.

"He had some problems with agoraphobia – you know, fear of open spaces? He's used to having his head covered with a helmet, or being in air town where they have a dome," Helene said.

"Air town?"

While Helene was explaining that to her parents, Tom rose quietly and walked to the window that faced east. The sky was dark, and the Moon was just rising, still orange from touching the horizon.

Tom watched a moment, then returned to the table. "Are you okay, Tom?" Helene asked.

"Yeah, I'm fine. Night is easier for me anyway."

"The Moon looks beautiful from here, doesn't it?"

"Actually, it does," Tom said. "I didn't think it would be that bright from the ground, under all the atmosphere and all. You know, the dust is really a dark gray color. It is smaller than I thought it would be. When you see pictures from Earth, they always make the Moon look bigger."

"What do you Moon Men go look at when you're on vacation?" Fred asked. "Mountains or something?"

"We don't," Tom said. "The truth is, we don't like the Moon much. We like living there, but the actual rock, it's not worth much." He looked at Helene. "It's a lot more fun to look at your daughter. I like doing that. I kind of am here on vacation, and she's the scenery." Helene smiled and looked away.

They ate dessert, small round loaves of Mexican flan with carmelized sugar topping, which Tom had baked to a crispy top in the broiler. Helene and Tom cleaned the table and expected to go sit in the living room, but her parents both stood to leave. "I'm sorry, honey, we have to get home," Deborah said. "Tom, thank you for a wonderful dinner. I hope we'll see you again."

"Thanks," her father said. "Great food, Tom. Helene, love you, sweetie." They left.

"What was that all about?" Tom asked. "I mean, I'm not sure I know about smells. Do I smell bad?"

"No, no, you're fine, especially since we took that shower together before dinner," Helene said. "Actually, you smell real good. No, it's just, my parents always do this to me."

They went into the living room anyway and sat on the couch. "Is this something horrible, like your parents don't actually like you?" Tom asked.

"Not that. It's just, they've always said they don't want to get too close to any of my boyfriends because then it bothers them when the boyfriend goes away."

"How many boyfriends have there been, that you introduced your folks to?"

"Four ... no, five, counting ... counting this one guy in high school who didn't know he was my boyfriend because I never told him. I'm not confessing to being a slut, Tom. I'm confessing to being really sucky at relationships. I keep trying to make it work and it never does, and my mother and father decided they couldn't keep up with me. If I ever get married, they might go all crazy and maybe stay to have a beer with us or something."

"Is that why you became a traveling salesman?"

"Probably. I mean, I had reasons to go for that career and it turns out I'm good at it, but yeah ... I like to have reasons to leave, any time I need one." She looked directly at him. "Can you go outside, do you think? We could sit outside, there's a bench in front of the building. It's romantic to look at the Moon together."

"Okay."

Helene retrieved the sweater she had loaned him, saying "It's fall. It's not real cold yet, but you probably want this after dark." She took his hand and led him outside. They sat facing the street, next to a tiny garden of flowers. The Moon, a little past full, had risen more and become silvery-white. "It's nice that it's cool and the mosquitoes are gone," Helene said. "A lot of times in the summer, you can't sit out here for more than a minute."

"Boy, that sounds icky," Tom said. "That's something that would sure take a lot of getting used to. I've never had to deal with bugs, never even seen any except in books. Every tourist who comes into air town gets fumigated for them, and of course Moon Men don't have them at all."

He looked at the Moon, then shook his head. "I'm sorry," he said, "but it just doesn't do much for me."

"Do you see the face of the Man in the Moon?"

"Nope. I've heard of that, never did understand it." He said, "This is nice, to be out here. Trees on the street, grass, cars go by every once in a while, people on the sidewalk. Air town doesn't have night, you know. This is a new thing for me." He took a deep breath.

"Come to the window, sweet is the night air!" Helene said.

"Um?"

"An old poem," Helene said.

"Do you know, as much as we like music, Moon Men don't really do poetry much. Just in school, actually."

"Why is that, do you think?"

"I don't know. We have song lyrics, but they're always love songs. I guess it's because nature is totally non-sensual for us," Tom said. "We're so rich some ways, and so pathetic other ways." He shivered.

"Do you want to sit on the steps, under the awning?" Helene asked. "It's sort of like having a roof overhead."

"No, I'm good," Tom said. "But hey, I want to look up, but I'm feeling unstable. Will you hold me so I don't fall over?"

"Of course."

Tom stood, and craned his neck to look directly upward. Helene stood with him and put an arm around his shoulders. It was a clear night, with a few clouds overhead reflecting the city lights. He said, "It's hard to see with the streetlights and all. There's one, two stars. Three, unless that's Jupiter or something." He turned around, Helene standing protectively next to him. "There's two more. Helene, there are five stars in the sky, plus the Moon."

"Chicago is a big city. Lots of lights. Also the moonlight washes out some stars."

"I don't really want to criticize, I just want you to know that the Moon has some advantages, too."

"Tom, seeing the Night sky from Sinus Amoris ... that will stay with me the rest of my life. I've never seen anything like that," Helene said.

Tom shivered again. "Honey, you're getting cold," Helene said. "It's not bad out here, it's just you're used to air town, where the temperature is exactly the same all the time, aren't you?"

"Never thought about it much, but I guess you're right."

"Do you want to go in?"

"Not yet." He turned and kissed her, then said "Okay, now we can go in."

"No, we can't," Helene said. She kissed him in return. "Okay, fair's fair. Now let's get you inside."

When they went back into her kitchen, Helene glanced at the sink and stifled a scream. "Tom! Spider!"

"What is it?"

"Spider on the sink. I hate spiders! Kill it for me, please! Grab one of the paper towels there. No, not a regular towel, then I'd have spider gook all over it. Yeah, that one." Tom wadded up a paper towel and slammed the sink once, twice, over and over while the small black spider scuttled this way and that. Finally he squashed it, folded the paper towel and wiped the sink with it, then discarded the towel.

"Yuck," he said. "Turns out I hate spiders, too. I just didn't know it until I saw one. Do they get in here very often?"

"No, no, hardly ever."

"Okay, so now you're supposed to throw yourself at me and say 'You saved my life! Take me!'"

"We already did that scene," Helene said. "Try to keep up, dear."

Tom led her back to the living room couch and they sat again. "I'll tell you what I'm trying to do," he said. "I'm trying to force the issue. Look, we've got one bad alternative where you move, or another bad alternative where I move, or a completely horrible alternative where we split up and we both lose. But we've got to do something. So let's pretend I just saved your life, so you throw yourself at me and move to the Moon and you can tell yourself 'I made the sacrifice but I did it for the relationship.' Or you do something like ... I don't know ... something that makes me say 'I'll make the sacrifice and live on Earth, because I'm doing it for the relationship.' I mean, there's no sense in both of us being heartbroken, when we can have a marriage where one of us feels resentful and the other one feels guilty. Even that's better than splitting up, right?"

"You sure sure know how to sweet-talk a girl, Romeo," she said. "Usually when a guy tries to talk a woman into something, it's to get her into a bed, not into a box. You know what I'm going to do? I'm going to sweet-talk you into bed. To sleep. That's what we need right now."

"Now that you mention it, it's been a long day, hasn't it?"

"It has," Helene said, pulling him up and embracing him. "But I wouldn't have missed it for the world. I'm glad you came here, even if it's going to end up hurting both of us. Now come on, we need sleep."

*   *   *

When she awoke in the morning, Helene was alone in her bed. She sat up and called "Tom!" without results. She searched the apartment, then put on a robe and went out into the building hallway.

Tom was sitting on the front steps, under the awning. It was raining gently. Helene went out and sat next to him. "Tom," she said, "you scared me, leaving me like that."

"I'm sorry, I'm sorry," he said. He glanced at her, but turned back to watch the falling rain. "I woke up

199

and looked out the window, and I couldn't help myself. I had to go out, and I didn't want to wake you. But, look at it. I had to be here. It's *rain*."

"Rain is nice," Helene said. "I like rain, as long as I'm under the awning and not out in it." She looked at him and realized the water on his face was not rain. He was crying. She put her arm around his shoulders.

"Smell the air," Tom said. "Isn't that delicious? I've never smelled air like that. I mean, I've smelled good smells and bad smells in the air, but this is the first time in my life I ever smelled air that smells good, itself. Does that make sense?"

"Don't they spray water on the crops, in air town?"

"I've never heard of that, it sounds wasteful. But if even if they did and even if I was there, it wouldn't smell like this and it wouldn't have the gray sky and this light and you wouldn't hear it hit the sidewalk and for sure, nobody would waste enough water to make puddles. Come on, let's go stand in it."

"Tom, kissing in the rain is one of the standard romantic things to do, but not in a bathrobe," Helene said, smiling. "It would get all soppy. You wait here while I go get my clothes. I won't be long."

"Are all women practical like that, during romantic moments?"

"Just the hopeless romantics," she said. "If I were more practical, I would have gotten dressed first. You wait here."

When she came back out, Tom gestured toward the street and said, "Look how the wind moves it. Little ripples that you can see where the rain hits the ground, heavier and then lighter. This is ... I don't have any words for what this is."

"This is a very ordinary rain storm on a very ordinary residential street in a pretty ordinary city," Helene said. "The only thing really special is you, dear. Out in the rain with you, now."

They walked two steps forward, stood on the sidewalk and kissed. "Do you know," Helene said, looking up at him, "I have never actually done the romantic-kiss-in-the-rain thing with anybody before. Just didn't happen to come up. I'm glad it was with you. I love you."

Tom said, "I love you. But we're getting wet and it's cold, so let's get back under the awning. How about a kiss under the awning? Ever had one of those?"

"I've lived in this apartment for seven years. Quit while you're ahead, darling." They sat back down on the steps.

"Helene, this is my second day on Earth. Look, don't get me in trouble for saying something else is wonderful besides you ..."

"I won't play that trick on you, Tom. Really, I won't."

"This rain is ... I'm crying again. I can't help it, between you and this air and the gray morning light, my heart is bursting. If this is ordinary, what is the rest of the Earth going to do to me?" He suddenly turned to her and said, "Your Mom said Lake Michigan is six blocks from here. When does it look most beautiful?"

"Sunrise, I guess. That's what everybody says, anyway. I saw the sun rising over the lake a couple of times in college, but not since then. And yeah, now that I remember, it was pretty nice."

"Take me there at sunrise."

"Okay. But Tom, it's not that urgent. The sun rises once a day, around these parts."

"I need to see something so beautiful I can't stand leaving it," Tom said. "I just figured this out. I suppose it should be the Grand Canyon or the Swiss Alps or Paris. One of the big tourist things that are supposed to be super-super beautiful."

"Tom," Helene interrupted him, "I've never seen any of those things myself."

"And I don't need to see them. The lake, the forest thing ..."

"Forest Preserve."

"Yeah, that. That stuff will be enough to knock me over. Don't you see, when I see those things, it will be impossible for me ever to leave Earth, so I don't have to make a decision. I stay here, I marry you, nobody has to feel resentful or guilty. I am a goddam genius at emotional logic. Problem solved."

"Tom," Helene said, "you don't have to marry me to get a day at the beach, or a walk in the woods. Anyway, I'm not sure I want to introduce you to a chick who might be a rival to me, even if it's Mother Nature."

"This is the way out of our dilemma," Tom said. "I fix it so I can't leave, nobody has to make a sacrifice and we live happily ever after. It's perfect."

"You haven't actually asked me to marry you yet."

"Oh," Tom said. "Helene, will you marry me?"

"Yes."

"Good."

"It is so hard," Helene said, raising her voice to an invisible audience, "to get men to remember their lines. Let's try this scene again, dear, and this time, stick to the script. Ready now? Lights, camera, action."

Tom stood, took her by both hands and led her the two steps back to the sidewalk. He took her face in his hands and kissed her. "Helene, I love you more than I can say. I mean literally, I can't say it. We're all supposed to be the big human relations experts on the Moon, but when I really need to say what I feel, I suddenly realize I don't know anything about love. Or Earth, or you, actually. I just want to spend the rest of my life learning."

"I don't know anything about love either. That's good. That's why I was still single when you came along. Tom, I love you and I don't need anything or anybody to confirm that. I know."

"I will always love you. So now I'm really asking, and I know it's a real question because all of a sudden I'm scared to death of what the answer might be. Helene, will you marry me?"

"Yes. Also yes for the next time you ask me."

"I get to do this again? I like doing this. This whole idea gets better and better."

"I'm counting on it. Years and years, you and me, getting better and better."

They kissed again, and presently had enough sense to come in out of the rain.

19: Helene Uses a Lot of Words

"Yeah, we're going to go to the beach in time for sunrise. But Tom, you are the worst schemer in the history of guys who think they're putting one over on credulous women. I'll tell you a secret — *we always know*. It just that sometimes, we decide to let you think you're fooling us."

"You're using a lot of words. We're still getting married, right?"

"Of course we're still getting married. But not because of this stupid trip to the lake. I know exactly what you're going to do when we get there. You're going to say 'Oh! I am overcome by beauty! I must stay on Earth forever now, so we will live our lives in love right here!' Probably after that you'll swoon, just for added drama."

"Helene, we don't have to go to the lake. It's four in the morning. We can get out of the car and go back to bed, and I'll still love you and I'll still stay with you forever."

"We'll do that in any event. But I figured out a way to force you to sell your spices to the ship's chandler companies and make enough money that I can earn a living as your salesman."

"On the Moon? We're going to be here. I was going to have my family sell the business. Anyway, I don't want to sell spices to tourists, they don't care what they eat as long as there's too much of it. How could you force me to sell to them?"

"I will bat my eyes and look up at you and say please, and you will do my bidding."

"Um … well, okay, that would work. But I thought you didn't want to go to the Moon."

"I heard from my old company. They've given all my accounts away to other salesmen, so if I went back, I'd have to start from scratch. If I'm going to start over, I want to do it with you, on the Moon. Selling stuff that tastes good."

"Well, that's a dumb reason. You could easily get a different job here."

"The other reason is, I think I finally understand why I'm so bad at relationships."

"You were with the wrong guys?"

"Never. They were all perfectly good men. Tom, one thing I finally figured out is that I want a man who will make any sacrifice to keep me, a man who will pay any price and do anything for my love. I want to be that valuable to somebody."

"Well, I think that's what I did offer you, isn't it?"

"You did. But Tom my very dearest, I don't need you to make the sacrifice. I just need you to make the offer. You've done that, in a way I can completely believe in."

"That still doesn't mean you have to go to the Moon."

"But it does. That was the other thing I figured out. I have to offer that sacrifice too. It doesn't work any other way. That's what I never did before. Tom, Tom, I will make any sacrifice to keep you, go anywhere, live in a tin can, let you lecture me about my blood-lipid levels. I will go to the Moon with you."

"Okay, I believe it. But as you say, you just have to make the offer. You don't have to do it."

"I don't know whether you would believe it or not, but I'm not sure I would believe that I was sincere in that offer unless I actually do it. So we're going home, your home, now our home."

"I wasn't kidding about crying from smelling the rain. It really hit me that hard."

"I know. I have utter faith that leaving Earth is going to cost you, dear. Leaving Earth is going to cost me, too. Don't have any doubt about that. By the way, I intend to make so much money selling spices to gobble-gobble tourists that we can afford to come back on vacation every once in a while. But do you see what will make this marriage work? We're both going for broke. We're in this together. Do you believe it?"

"Yes. Kiss me."

"Um. Okay, now we can go to the beach. Here's a tip – walk far enough out on the beach that when you swoon, you hit your head on the soft sand. It'll save you a headache."

"Will the sunrise be as beautiful as you?"

"Probably more beautiful, but I'm more fun to roll around with in the sand."

20: Suns and Raindrops

The wedding parade stepped off at exactly eighteen minutes to sunset, from the outskirts of Sinus Amoris village, a time calculated precisely by the wedding planner the Easterday family had hired. The bride and groom wore suits decorated with stylized suns, with patches of brown paper over their hearts. They had decided not to require any uniform dress for the Maid of Honor (Yeni), the five bridesmaids (the only five women Helene had substantially met on her first visit), the Best Man (Gregor), the groomsmen (all relatives of Tom) and the assorted cute toddlers, all of whose mothers had dressed their suits up in bright colors anyway. They danced to the music provided by the band and waved to the crowds along the streets, heading for the First Baptist Church.

The sunshades began to come down in the village, folding up, rolling up, settling down. At the precise moment the parade entered the church, the sun set, and the Night sky unveiled its benediction on them. The Earth was a sliver in the sky, blue and white and warm.

The minister stepped up to perform the ceremony. Tom and Helene held hands, then peeled off their brown stickers to reveal the shared symbol they had chose to represent their marriage to others. It was a pattern of rain drops, a stylized image which was not familiar to Moon Men and which they would have to explain over and over. They recited a little speech, alternating lines, about how they would refresh and nourish each other, wet down their marriage with shared tears of joy and sorrow, be grateful for the blessings that fall from the heavens, and other even sappier sentiments. Both of Tom's parents cried noisily, and Helene's parents also cried, on a telephone link with a one-and-a-quarter second delay. The wedding planner distributed their weeping to everyone.

The crowd pulled back to open up the dance floor. The groom's attendants picked up Tom, the bridesmaids picked up Helene, and they were thrown into the sky as the band began to play.

They met at the apogee, grasped hands and whirled around their common center of gravity. They settled slowly down and their feet touched the lunar ground ...

... to begin their dance together!

Afterword

I want to give some credit to the books and movies I learned from while working on this novel. A *lot* of the background on space suits comes from Nicholas de Monchaux's book *Spacesuit: Fashioning Apollo* (MIT Press, 2011). This is a really wonderful history of the spacesuits developed for the Gemini and Apollo programs, centered on the interesting fact that the suits that wound up being used were not made by aerospace contractors. They were made by a division of Playtex, the bra and girdle people. The aerospace guys were very scornful of the idea of trusting something made by women with sewing machines to protect an astronaut from vacuum, but the plain fact is that every time they did a comparison test, the Playtex suits fit better and were preferred by the astronauts. I decided to give my Moon Men suits that look something like the Litton Industries RX2A suit (you can search on that name if you're interested in a picture).

I also made heavy use of Marshall T. Savage's *The Millenial Project* (Little, Brown & Company,

1994). This is a swell resource for any SF writer, and a lot of my background on Moon crater cities and mass drivers comes from it. Another helpful book was Antonín Rükl's *Atlas of the Moon* (Kalmbach Books, 1992). Theophrastus Crater met my need for a crater city exactly: it's small, round, has a cool ancient Greek name and intact walls and is right next to a big flat area that would be perfect for a spaceport. The fact that "Sinus Amoris" means "Bay of Love" was just a bonus.

Naturally, as a science fiction writer I also had to re-read Robert Heinlein's *Have Space Suit, Will Travel*, *The Menace from Earth* and *The Moon is a Harsh Mistress*, as well as a bunch of other Moon books by other SF writers. (There is some possibility I was just dodging work while reading these books.)

Romantic comedy is preeminently a movie genre, so of course I watched a lot of rom-coms, particularly that sub-genre of a man and woman from different cultures learning to adapt to one another. Three favorites I can recommend: *Fools Rush In* (1997: An American man – Matthew Perry – meets a Mexican woman – Salma Hayek). *The Other End of the Line* (2009: An American man – Jesse Metcalfe – meets an Indian woman – Shriya Saran). *Tim Burton's Corpse Bride* (2005: A living man – Johnny Depp – meets a dead woman – Helena Bonham Carter. A favorite line – Victor: This could never work out. Don't you see, you're dead? Emily: You should have thought of that before you asked me to marry you!)

Although my Moon Men are foodies, I am not, really. But I have been trying out recipes for "meatballs and little chunky things," as Helene says, and I can recommend Rick Rodgers' cookbook *I Love Meatballs!* (Andrews McMeel Publishing, 2011). I particularly like his chicken meatballs with fresh ginger, although he has an elaborate recipe for home-made teriyaki sauce involving mirin (a sweetened Japanese rice wine) and three other ingredients, but I just use what I can buy in a bottle. They're still good.

And of course I need to thank my wife Kathie for her support, and for teaching me about love. Thanks to my beta readers, particularly Deborah, Donna, Darcie, Kim and Mike, and thanks to all my friends who've let me rattle on about this project.

See more at http://CharlesOtt.com.

Colophon

The text font is *Linden Hill* by Barry Schwartz, which is a re-cutting of Frederic Goudy's *Deepdene*. I obtained this font from The League of Moveable Type.